ISHMAEL
AND THE
RETURN
OF THE
DUGONGS

ISHMAEL
AND THE
RETURN
OF THE
DUGONGS

MICHAEL GERARD BAUER

templar

A TEMPLAR BOOK

First published by Omnibus Books,
an imprint of Scholastic Australia Pty Ltd, 2007

Published in the UK in 2012 by Templar Publishing,
an imprint of The Templar Company Limited,
The Granary, North Street, Dorking, Surrey,
RH4 1DN, UK

www.templarco.co.uk

Cover design by crushed.co.uk

First UK edition

ISBN 978-1-84877-712-5

Printed and bound by CPI Group (UK) Ltd,
Croydon, CR0 4YY

To my father-in-law
L.P.J. 'Ben' van Schyndel (1925–2006)
Master tradesman, artist, philosopher,
knight in shining white overalls
and tireless promoter of my books.
With love and thanks.

CONTENTS

Track 1:
Collision Course

Track 2:
Dead Toad Society Blues

Track 3:
Each and Every Line

Track 4:
Pain

Track 5:
Memory Sea

Track 6:
All the Time

Track 7:
Bad Day for Angels

Track 8:
The Time has Come

Track 9:
The Very Best of Everything

Track 1:
Collision Course

I'm tracking you down
I'm hot on your trail
Girl, I got you square in my sights
I'm zeroing in
You're glowing on my radar
Flashing like a warning light

Chorus
Collision course
We're headed for a showdown
There's nothing that can keep us apart
Collision course
There's just no way around it
You're coming head to head with my heart

From The Dugongs: *Returned & Remastered*
Music & lyrics: W. Mangan and R. Leseur

1.
Welcome to My Nightmare

The phone growled in my ear like an angry bear. I crashed it back down. I picked it up. *Grrrrrrrrrrrrrrrrrrrrrrrrr!* I crashed it down.

Welcome to my nightmare.

For the hundredth time I ran through the three items on my checklist.

1. Kelly Faulkner.

This was to remind me who I was phoning just in case my brain suddenly turned into Play Dough. Don't laugh. This was a definite possibility. After all, I was phoning Kelly Faulkner – and not just *any* Kelly Faulkner, but Kelly Faulkner of the ice-blue eyes and the cute white teeth, Kelly Faulkner of the 'only in my dreams' body and the heart-attack smile. Yes, that's right – *that* Kelly Faulkner. Breathtakingly, mind-meltingly, jaw-droppingly, brain-bubblingly, stomach-churningly, heart-poundingly perfect Kelly Faulkner.

No pressure.

I moved down the list.

2. Ishmael Leseur.

That's me. It's also the name of a frightening but as yet virtually unknown medical condition. And if you're thinking it's pretty stupid writing your own name down so that you can remember it, then you've obviously never suffered from Ishmael Leseur's Syndrome. (Which I guess is hardly surprising, since I'm the world's only known case.) But what you have to realise is that something like making a phone call to Kelly Faulkner is *just* the kind of situation where the main symptom of Ishmael Leseur's – rampant stupidity on a massive scale – is most likely to flare up. And I'm warning you, from my vast experience, you don't want to be around if it does.

Last year I had some truly awful attacks. I even wrote a scientific report documenting every humiliating second of it. The thing was, though, by the end of the year I really started to believe that I had the worst of Ishmael Leseur's Syndrome under control. After all, didn't I sort of rescue some primary kid from being picked on by the resident school bully Barry Bagsley? And didn't that kid turn out to be Kelly Faulkner's (yes, *that* Kelly Faulkner's) little brother? And because of that, didn't Kelly Faulkner, girl of my dreams, invite me and my mate Razza to her friend's birthday party so that now all I had to do was ring her up to accept and my life would be perfect? All true.

Which brings me to the last item on the list.

3. Party.

My planning and attention to detail were legendary. I was expecting a job offer from the Mission Impossible Force any minute now. Nothing had been left to chance. I knew the routine off by heart. All I had to do was plug in the number and when someone answered I'd say, "Hi, can I speak to (checking the list)... *Kelly* please?" If/when Kelly picked up I'd say, "Hi, Kelly, it's (checking the list again)... *Ishmael Leseur* here, just ringing about the (checking the list one more time) ... *party*."

Yes, the list was an absolute good. It was a thing of beauty, stunning in its simplicity. Not only that, it was totally foolproof. There was just one nagging question left unanswered. Was it Ishmael-Leseur-Syndrome-proof?

Now that was a tough one. To fully appreciate the awful burden that is Ishmael Leseur's Syndrome you'd have to read the detailed report I compiled last year, only I don't suppose you could, seeing as how there's only one copy and it's been buried under a pile of shoes at the bottom of my cupboard, or at least it was until I accidentally mentioned it to my English teacher Miss Tarango. Then, before I knew it, she was asking me if she could read it. Of course I wanted to say, "No way!", but hey, it was Miss Tarango, and she's the best teacher I've ever had and she's got this way of looking at you and these cute little cheeks and these dimples and... well... I handed it over.

Not all of it, of course – just a sample. (There was some detailed scientific analysis concerning Kelly

Faulkner and Miss Tarango herself that was classified 'Highly Confidential'.) The weird thing was, Miss really liked the bit she read. Who'd have thought an English teacher would be interested in scientific reports? She even talked about showing it to some people she knew – doctors, I guess. Who knows, maybe my report could be published in some big medical journal and Ishmael Leseur's Syndrome will finally get the recognition it so richly deserves.

The other thing Miss Tarango asked me to do was to write another report on this year. So that's what I'm doing. For reasons – see above re cheeks and dimples (by the way, the aforementioned 're' is an excellent word to include in a report, as is 'aforementioned').

To tell you the truth, I was kind of hoping that there wouldn't be much to write about this time around. Like I said, when Kelly Faulkner invited me to her friend's party, I really thought that maybe I was finally getting on top of Ishmael Leseur's Syndrome and that this year was going to be a much smoother ride.

Not even close.

That 'smooth ride' I was hoping for turned out to be a roller coaster on growth hormones. You know, one of those wild gut-wrenchers that hurtle you towards total annihilation while your internal organs feel as if they're being rearranged by a madman with a shovel and which usually ends with your digestive system thrusting itself into full-throttle reverse.

But I'm getting way ahead of myself now. Miss Tarango's got this thing about the importance of organisation and planning. She says that everything you write should have a clear beginning, middle and end.

So here are mine.

Beginning: The very start of the year at St Daniel's Boys College.

Middle: The aforementioned roller coaster ride on growth hormones.

End: The night that The Dugongs returned.

There, that doesn't sound too terrible, does it? And it all starts off innocently enough. Geez, all I had to do was make a simple phone call.

2.
R-Rated Cluedo

It was ringing. I could hear myself breathing in the earpiece. Why couldn't she have given me her email address or her mobile number, so I could just text? Perhaps no one was home. One more ring and I'd hang up.

Suddenly the line clunked and rattled and a man's voice answered. "Hello. Faulkner's Fried Food and Funeral Parlour. *You die – we fry.* How may I help you?"

"What? I... ah... I thought... Sorry... I... ah... There must be... I wanted... I think I got the wrong number."

"That's not Macca, is it? Sorry about that. Just joking. I was expecting someone else. Dave Faulkner here.

Who are you after?"

"I… ah… I." The list! I snatched it up. "Um… *Kelly*… Could I speak to Kelly, please?"

"Kelly? Just hold on a tick and I'll check. I think she might be in the shower."

In the *shower*? Kelly Faulkner? (*Warning! Potential sensory overload!*) Kelly Faulkner… in the *shower*. Kelly Faulkner… in the shower… with the *soap suds*. It was like an R-rated version of Cluedo. I had to get my mind back on the job. I desperately scanned my checklist. *Kelly – Ishmael – Party*. Forget the shower thing. *Kelly – Ishmael – Party*. Don't think about the shower thing. *Kelly – Ishmael – Party*. Don't think of Kelly Faulkner lathered up like she's in one of those shampoo commercials – closing her eyes and smiling as she rinses the suds from her hair while the water trickles and bubbles over her face and shoulders and the camera sloooowly pans down… (*Danger! System overheating!*) The list! Concentrate on the list! *Kelly – Ishmael – Party*. Okay. *Kelly – Ishmael – Party*. All right. *Kelly – Ishmael – Party*. That's better. *Kelly – Ishmael…*

Clunk. Rattle. "She won't be long. Who should I say is calling?"

"… *Party*."

"Paddy? Well hang on, Paddy, she'll be with you shortly."

"No… No, wait… It's Ishmael… Ishmael Leseur…"

But it was too late – a voice was now calling out in the background, "Kel, it's a *Paddy* someone… Yeah, I'm sure that's what he said."

Great. Now she'll think I'm an Irish stalker. I tried to calm myself down. Not an easy task with my heart giving an inspired beatbox performance in my chest.

Muffled sounds came down the line.

I tried to imagine the scene at the other end. What did their house look like? Where was the phone? In the kitchen? In the lounge room? Maybe they had a cordless phone. Maybe Kelly would take it into her room… after she got out of the shower… wrapped in a towel. Just think, the only thing between Kelly Faulkner's bare flesh and me would be a thin cotton towel… that and a mere six or seven kilometres of telephone cable. Anyone for Cluedo? Kelly Faulkner… in her *bedroom*… with a *towel*… With *just* a towel.

"Hello?"

"Kelly? Hi, ah… it's (*checking the list*) Ishmael…

Ishmael Leseur here." All right, I could do this. The trick was to remain focused. "Just ringing about the towel."

"Ishmael? Sorry, what... what was that about a towel?"

"No... I... ah... I... It must be a bad line... Nothing about a *towel*... No... I was just saying... that I was ringing... to... *tell*... you that I got your letter... and Razza and I can come to Sally's party." Brilliant!

"Oh... right... Well that's good, that's great."

Phew. Okay, I was in the clear.

"So... why did you tell my dad that your name was Paddy?"

Then again. "I... ah... I... It's... It's just... It's a nickname."

"Your nickname is *Paddy*?"

"Well... not *exactly*. I'm... just sort of... trying it out, you know, to see if it works or not."

"Why Paddy?"

"Ah... It's a long story." (Yes, it starts way back when I was born with an overactive stupidity gland.)

"Is your family Irish?"

"Ah... well... Yeah, sort of."

"*Leseur* doesn't sound very Irish."

"No… It's… probably from Mum's side of the family."

"Right… so what was your mum's name?"

Hey, any time anyone wants to lend me a hand here that would be great – you know it can get pretty tiring digging your own grave.

"Umm… I'm not *really* sure."

"You don't know what your mum's name was before she was married?"

"Well… I do… I just can't think of it. I know it sounded pretty Irish, though… Something like… um… Bono… but I could be wrong."

"Bono? What, like Bono from U2?"

"Well something *like* that, but probably not *that* exactly. I'm not really sure. Anyway, I don't really think *Paddy* suits me. I'll probably forget about it."

"Good move," Kelly said with a bit of a laugh.

Then the line went silent. I had to say something to fill the gap – something clever, something witty, something sophisticated.

"Yeah," I said. Well, what did you expect from someone with a Play Dough brain?

"Right, well anyway, that's great that you can both

come to the party. I'll get Sally to send you an invitation with all the details on it. It's just going to be a barbecue at her house with her family, but it should be fun. There's about six or seven girls coming from school and about the same number of guys including you two. Oh, and Sally said not to worry about presents, but to bring your trunks because there's a pool."

"Great." Yes, I was thrilled – me in my trunks. At last the steroids and all the hours in the gym pumping iron were going to pay off. I just hoped that Kelly and the other girls wouldn't be too overwhelmed by the sight of my rippling muscles and forget that there was a sensitive, weedy stick figure of a guy under all that beefy bulk.

"Look, sorry to rush off, but I better go. I'm just out of the shower and I'm dripping all over the floor." (*Error: This program has performed an illegal operation and will shut down.*)

"Ishmael? Ishmael, are you still there?"

"What? Oh yeah… I'm here." I wasn't really, though. I was off on Fantasy Island playing R-rated Cluedo.

"Well I guess I'll see you at Sally's, then. Bye, Ishmael… or should that be Paddy?"

"No… No, you can call me Ishmael."

"To be sure, to be sure," Kelly Faulkner said with a giggle, before adding, "See ya."

"Bye…"

I hung up the phone and stared at my checklist. *Kelly – Ishmael – Party.* Yes, it had gone like clockwork. I hope those Mission Impossible guys were listening in. They'll probably want me to head up their Australian bureau. Well, maybe not, but what did I care? *Kelly – Ishmael – Party.* That said it all, really. In about three weeks' time I was going to a party and Kelly Faulkner would be there. Everything was going to work out just great, I told myself.

You know, looking back, I think that was the moment when I should have signed myself up for Optimists Anonymous. I could have attended meetings with people like that guy in *King Kong* who said, "Sure, let's take the gigantic killer ape to New York – what could possibly go wrong?"

3.
The Old Laid-back Approach

"She told you she was only wearing a towel?" We were in our form room. It was Monday morning, the first day back at St Daniel's Boys College, and most of the class was still slowly drifting in.

I stopped unpacking my bag and studied the two big eyes and the open mouth that hovered before me like three-fifths of the Olympic rings.

They belonged to Orazio Zorzotto, aka Razz, Razza, or the Razzman (only one poor, misguided fool ever used the term *the Big Z*).

"She didn't actually *say* she was only in a towel. She just said she was dripping all over the floor."

"Mate, if she just got out of the shower and she's dripping on the floor, then either she's in a towel or she's… *Maaaaaaaaate*! You are *so* in. You're laughing. Shut the gate, dude – you are home and hosed!"

"Razz, what are you talking about?"

"Look, you think she just *happened* to be in the shower when you rang?"

"Yes."

"Yeah, well, maybe. But do you think it was an accident that she just *happened* to let slip that she was standing there half-naked?"

"But she didn't say that."

"Look Ishmael, it's the Razzman you're talking to here – the Big Z – and I know chicks, right?"

Now this was a debatable point. Razza certainly *talked* a lot about 'chicks' and he obviously *thought* a lot about 'chicks', but as for actually *knowing* anything, well, the jury was still out on that one. I was about to raise these very valid concerns when he ploughed on.

"… and I'm telling you, this is what chicks do. She's sending you a subtle message, man. You gotta get the radar going here. You gotta pick up on these things. Do you think if she was on the phone to the local priest she'd say, 'Hi, Father, lovely to talk to you; by the way, do you realise I'm standing here totally starkers at the moment?' No way. Man, she's got the hots for you – bad. You are *so* in, dude!"

"Razz, I think you're getting a bit carried away."

What was I saying? 'Carried away' was the Razza's natural state. It was like pointing out to a hurricane that it was being a touch breezy.

"You'll see, man. Just wait till the party. You and Kelly Faulkner – *wicked*!"

In the seat beside me, Orazio Zorzotto drummed a manic beat on the lid of the desk while his head bobbed up and down and his legs jumped like crazy.

"Look, Razza… about the party… Just don't… you know… just don't go crazy with this 'me and Kelly Faulkner' thing, okay? I mean, don't make a big deal out of it, all right? I just want her to think that I'm *normal* for a change, that's all. So don't go acting… you know… like a madman or anything."

Razza stopped drumming and pushed his fingers through his mess of black hair so that it stuck up at strange angles. "I get it. What you're saying is, you want me to be sort of low-key… a little… inconspicuous…

Adopt the old laid-back approach."

"Yeah… laid-back. That'd be good."

Razza raised his eyebrows, pushed out his bottom lip and nodded thoughtfully. "Yeah… sure… No worries. I'm totally cool with that."

"Thanks," I said, starting to feel a little less stressed about the party. It lasted around fifteen seconds. As I leaned over to drag the remaining books from my school bag, a sharp jab hit my ribs. I turned around to find Razza's face leering at me.

"Eh… Kelly Faulkner," he said sticking out his tongue and panting. "What d'ya reckon, eh?" My ribs suffered another onslaught. "You and Kelly Faulkner? Kel-ly Faulk-ner," he repeated like a deranged hypnotist while his eyes grew into two big satellite dishes. "You da man, Ishmael," he said, punching my shoulder. "Just think, you and Kelly Faulkner… you and the Kel-ster… the Kel-meister… the Kel-enheimer!"

Razza shouted this last title as if he was introducing a boxing match and accompanied it with such a thunderous drum roll on the desktop that everyone stopped what they were doing and stared as his hands blurred into a flurry of blows. It was only a matter of time before either Razza or the desk exploded into flames. That was until...

"Mr Zorzotto! Cease and desist!"

Immediately the room transformed into a living display of wax dummies that would have made Madame Tussaud weep with envy. Every sound, every movement, every breath, every spark of life had been swallowed by a black hole that now hovered menacingly in the doorway. It was the Deputy Principal, Mr Barker, and he was glaring at Razza, who now sat with his hands frozen mid-beat just centimetres off the desk.

"I generally try to avoid executing anyone on the first day of a new school year, Mr Zorzotto," he said in a grinding growl. "It tends to unsettle the younger students. However, as I consider you a very *special* case, I am willing to make an exception."

Listening to Mr Barker chew out his words always made me think of a car being slowly crushed into scrap metal by a steel vice.

"So I want to make it *perfectly* clear to you, Mr Zorzotto, that if you so much as brush your little pinky against that desk one more time, you will find yourself experiencing something that will make the unspeakable horrors of the Spanish Inquisition seem like a therapeutic massage. Do we understand each other?"

Razza moved his head up and down in slow motion as if he knew that one false move was sudden death.

"Wonderful," Mr Barker said, then threw one last sweeping glare at the rest of us before stalking off.

I waited a few seconds then let out my breath. Around me signs of life began to seep back into the room. I checked Razza. He still hadn't moved a muscle.

"Razz, he's gone."

He rotated stiffly in my direction. His face was as blank as an empty page and his arms still hovered zombie-like in front of him.

"Razz? You okay?"

For a moment there was no reaction, then the mouth before me slid into a cheesy grin and a pair of eyes lit up like demented mirror balls. "Kelly Faulkner," Razza whispered, "the Big Kel – huna!"

Then he beat out the remainder of his furious drum roll on the top of my head.

Yep… the old laid-back approach… The Razzman was totally cool with that.

4.
Fish-whale and the Rebut-heads

"**H**ey, where's Scobie, anyway?" Razza asked after he had finished using my skull as a bongo drum.

I'd been wondering the same thing. "Don't know. He was supposed to be here from the first day."

A few more boys wandered into the room. One of them was Ignatius Prindabel.

"Yo Prindabel – my main man," Razza called.

A thin stooping figure looked up, nodded and loped his way awkwardly towards us. "Leseur. Zorzotto," he said, then shoved his fists into his pockets and studied us silently as if we were specimens in a lab.

Razza held up his hands. "Whoa, steady on,

how about letting someone else get a word in once in a while?"

Ignatius stared back at Razza like he always did – as if he was looking at some bizarre abstract painting whose meaning and purpose completely escaped him. I couldn't blame him: they didn't have much in common. Razz was sort of "out there" while Ignatius was more 'along the corridor, down the stairs and tucked away in the far corner of the basement'.

"So Prindabel, tell me, what exciting things did you get up to over the holidays, eh? Steam-clean your calculator? Fumigate the encyclopedias perhaps? Try out for the lead role in the local musical production of *Revenge of the Nerds*?"

"Actually," Prindabel said, "I attended the Junior University Maths and Science Summer School programme."

"Of *course* you did," Razza said. "And I was going to do that as well, but then I decided it would be more fun if I just inserted bamboo shoots under my fingernails and watched some grass grow."

Ignoring Razza completely, Prindabel turned to me. "Did you know that at the Central Missouri State

University they've just identified the largest Mersenne prime number ever? It's 9.8 million digits long – that's two to the 32,582,657th power minus one. They had to use 700 computers! Can you believe it?"

I shook my head. I couldn't believe it.

"Man, you must be dynamite on a date, Prindabel," Razza said. "I can see you now: 'Tell me, sweetheart, would you like to check out my Mersenne prime? It's 9.8 million digits long, you know.'"

Ignatius gave Razza another of his 'abstract painting' looks, then shrugged his shoulders and glanced around the room. "Scobie's not here," he said.

"Oh, well done, Sherlock," Razza said. What tipped you off? Was it the fact that he's not here? You should have your own *CSI* spin-off series. *CSI Nerd*."

Just then the large form of Bill Kingsley ambled into the classroom. "Billy-boy, over here. Hey, have you been on a diet or what?"

"Maybe."

"I think another pizza and movie marathon night at your place might be in order. You know, Bilbo, if you lose any more weight they'll downgrade you to a small planet. Then watch out, man. You saw what happened to Pluto."

Bill gave a slight smile. "Where's Scobie?"

"Not sure yet, but we should have something soon. Prindabel's leading the crime scene investigation team. He's just waiting on forensics."

A scuffle at the door caught our attention. Doug Savage and Danny Wallace were wrestling over a football until Danny finally wrenched it free and charged to the back of the room with Doug in hot pursuit.

Moments later a solid figure with a helmet of blonde hair and a snarl appeared. Have you met Barry Bagsley, talented sportsperson, professional bully, prince of the put-down and dictator-in-waiting? He surveyed the room before pushing his way through a group of boys and heading in the direction of Danny and Doug, who were happily thumping into each other in the back row. Unfortunately he stopped when he came to us.

"Well, if it isn't the famous debating girls – Fish-whale and the Rebut-heads."

Rebut-heads – that was new. Barry must have been honing his skills over the holidays. Then he looked at Bill and sneered. "You know, Kingsley, they reckon you are what you eat. So what did you eat, eh? A herd of pigs?"

Bill's eyes dropped, but he said nothing.

"So what's your favourite meal, then? Beef jerky?"

Barry Bagsley's smile slid into a snarl. "Well, it looks like funny man Zor-*zit*-to has something to say. You know, Or-*arse*-i-*hole*, you should be very careful. Someday someone might take your jokes the wrong way and you'll end up with your nose spread all over your face."

"Just trying to bring a little sunshine into an otherwise bleak and thankless world," Razza said with a smile.

Barry slowly prised his eyes away from Razz and turned to me. "And what have you got to say for yourself, Le Sewer? Nothin' as usual? Well, I haven't forgotten our little discussion at the end of last year, and I reckon you got some serious payback coming your way." He looked around the class. "No Scobie yet, Le Spewer? Gee, whose skirt are you gonna hide behind if *he* doesn't turn up?"

"I'm not hiding," I managed to mumble.

"Brave words, Manure," Barry laughed, "but we'll see – I promise you that. We will *definitely* see."

We all watched as he wandered to the back of the room, wrenched the football away from Danny Wallace and began twirling it on one finger.

"Gee, you know, I'd forgotten how much I missed Bagsley's little pep talks," Razza said. "Now I feel I'm ready to face the day!"

"You might just wanna watch what you say, Razz. I don't think he was joking about that nose thing."

"Look, man, I'm not stupid. Bagsley's dumb but he's not an idiot."

"What?"

"Well, he's never going to actually hit anyone, is he? Not at school, anyway. Man, can you imagine what would happen? After all the trouble he's been in can you imagine what Barker would do to him? They'd probably chuck him out. Bagsley knows that. Nah, if he was gonna biff anyone, it'd be somewhere away from the school, somewhere deserted."

"Well, I wouldn't get him too riled up."

"Yeah, well, what about you, dude? What was all the crap he was going on about 'payback' time? What did you do to him, anyway?"

"Nothing."

That wasn't entirely true. But I didn't feel like talking about last year's end-of-school assembly when I'd threatened to expose Barry Bagsley as a bully because he was making Bill's life hell. That's when I said that I wasn't going to hide from him any more – that next year I was going to stand up for myself. Well now it *was* next year, and I was struggling to picture myself actually doing that. On the other hand, picturing myself with my nose spread all over my face was a cinch.

I stole a glimpse at Barry Bagsley. His chair was tilted at a dangerous angle and he was rocking back and forth, butting the back of his head lightly against the rear wall. I wondered what was going on inside that head. He was probably devising new ways to indulge his favourite pastimes – advanced lesson disruption, random acts of torment, applied character assassination and creative bodily noises. Or maybe he was just like the rest of us, wondering where James Scobie was.

You really had to hand it to Scobie: he'd been at St Daniel's for less than a year, and yet in that time he'd taken on Barry Bagsley and won, inspired our struggling senior rugby team to a famous victory over arch-rivals Churchill Grammar and single-handedly dragged the first debating team in the school's history to the semi-finals. As a result, he'd become something of a cult hero with a reputation for being totally fearless. Not even the brain tumour scare that caused him to miss the last term of school had put a dent in him. In the testosterone-charged world of St Daniel's Boys College you just didn't get much bigger than James Scobie.

"Wow, it must be my lucky day. I haven't seen so many handsome faces in one place since I gatecrashed the *Cleo* Bachelor of the Year finals."

Miss Tarango stood beaming at us with her double-dimpled smile, her shiny blonde hair and her glowing beach-holiday skin. Was there ever a better sight in front of a classroom?

"Welcome back, boys. What do you say we get this show on the road? Danny, how about you put that football in your bag before it gets lost... permanently. Okay, let's quieten down, everyone. That's better. All right, gentlemen, before I bury you under a veritable mountain of administrivia I would just like to say how happy I am to be..."

Miss Tarango stopped and turned towards the door, where a small, pale boy had suddenly appeared. Everything about him was neat, even and tucked in. He looked like some primary kid playing dress up. Long grey socks stretched from the mirror-polish of his shoes to his knobbly knees and a pair of carefully pressed shorts rode high over the small mound of his belly. Behind the thin, round glasses that rested on his pink and slightly chubby cheeks, two dark pupils gazed calmly ahead. Then he squeezed his eyes shut and stretched them open while his lips rotated around bizarrely as if they were trying to escape his face.

Miss Tarango placed her hand high on her chest. "Well, boys, here's a sight to warm our hearts," she said, and a chorus of greetings and cheers bounced around the room as James Scobie smiled and waddled in.

5.
The 'S' Word

"Hey, Scobie. What's it like having someone screwing around in your brain?"

Registration was over and we were preparing for the next lesson. Miss Tarango had already left and Barry Bagsley, having fired off the first shot, was basking in the appreciative smirks of Danny Wallace and Doug Savage.

Scobie looked up. "I can't say that I'd recommend it. But at least it's something you'll never have to worry about. Your brain is safe. I don't think they've invented an electron microscope that powerful yet."

Barry Bagsley darkened like a thundercloud.

"Yeah well, just keep away from me, will ya? I wouldn't want to *catch* anything from you."

"You've got nothing to worry about," Scobie said pleasantly. "There's absolutely no scientific evidence at all of human-to-animal transmission."

When it came to a war of words between James Scobie and Barry Bagsley, it was never in doubt where the weapons of mass destruction were stored. But Scobie's power over Barry wasn't due only to his verbal skills, or even because the First Fifteen rugby team had adopted him as their mascot after a poem he wrote last year inspired them to conquer Churchill Grammar. No, it had more to do with Scobie's complete lack of fear, and his refusal to back down. The effect of Scobie's return on Barry Bagsley was the same as a muzzle being strapped on a mad dog.

Apart from having a more subdued bully, the new school year at St Daniel's Boys College started pretty much in the usual way. First we had the routine talks about how "crucial" this year was going to be and how we had to "knuckle down" to our study "right from the word go". Then each of our subject teachers outlined the work we were going to cover while at the same time trying to make it sound far more interesting than it really was and about as essential to our futures as learning how to breathe. As it turned out, Miss Tarango had the hardest battle in that regard.

"Boys, this term, as well as a class novel and a short Media unit, our main focus will be poetry."

Groans rose, eyes bulged, brows furrowed, heads dropped, and the entire class seemed to sag as if it had taken a collective blow to the stomach. Ignatius Prindabel wore the expression of someone who had recently been informed that he'd have to have his appendix removed via his backside.

Miss Tarango just smiled sweetly and ploughed on regardless. "Yes, this term we will have the opportunity of exploring and experiencing language at its most creative and powerful. We'll be looking at everything from song lyrics and rap to all sorts of poetry, starting with the classic love sonnets of Shakespeare."

The class froze and stared at Miss Tarango in horror. She'd said the S-word. Ignatius Prindabel went white and clutched his calculator to his chest as if someone had threatened to steal his favourite teddy.

Razza was the first to regain the ability to speak.

"Shakespeare! What do we have to do that for? Poetry's bad enough. Why can't we just stick with modern stuff? What are we doing Shakespeare for, Miss?" Nodding heads and rumblings of support filled the room.

Miss Tarango held up her hands, closed her eyes and waited for silence. When it returned, she opened her eyes, smiled at Razza and took a deep breath.

"In answer to your question," she said calmly, "we are doing Shakespeare, Orazio, because we wish to celebrate the very pinnacle of human thought. We are doing Shakespeare because we are bold and perceptive seekers of beauty and truth. In short, we are doing Shakespeare, Orazio, because we are lovers of life and language."

For a moment Razza seemed hypnotised by Miss Tarango's voice. Then he broke away and looked around the class. "We don't sound much like us."

"Well perhaps, Orazio," Miss Tarango said, raising her eyebrows, "*we* will surprise *us*."

Razza glanced across the aisle to where a cross-eyed Jarrod McGucken was attempting to pop a pimple on the end of his nose.

"I wouldn't get your hopes up too high if I were you, Miss," Razza said.

But Miss Tarango was having none of it. "Come on, boys," she pleaded. "Don't let me down here. We're St Daniel's men, remember – 'courage forged in a lion's den' and all that. James, you're on my side, aren't you? Give us the Scobie scoop on Shakespeare."

Scobie went through his usual facial stretches and contortions before he gave his considered reply. "*He was a man, take him for all in all. We shall not look upon his like again.*"

Miss Tarango pressed her lips into a tight line that made her dimples appear like magic. Then she swept her right hand grandly towards the small figure in front of her. "*What a piece of work is a Scobie. How noble in reason. How infinite in faculty. In form, in moving, how express and admirable!*"

James Scobie pulled nervously at the knot of his tie, lightly fingered the perfect swell of his gelled-back hair, carefully adjusted his glasses and blushed. Miss Tarango just smiled. The rest of us tried to work out what the hell they'd been talking about. Whatever it was, it seemed to have given Miss a new surge of energy and enthusiasm.

"Yes, poetry and Shakespeare it is, boys, in all their raging glory," she said with flashing eyes. "Bring it on!"

6.
A Child of the Universe

And bring it on Miss Tarango did. In the very next lesson the first of the posters went up. In big red print it said:

> ... *that which we are, we are;*
> *One equal temper of heroic hearts,*
> *Made weak by time and fate, but strong in will*
> *To strive, to seek, to find, and not to yield.*
> 'Ulysses', ALFRED, LORD TENNYSON, 1809–92

But that was only the beginning. Over the next couple of weeks Miss began to plaster every available square centimetre of classroom space with posters and printouts of poetry and song lyrics. Prindabel became so rattled he spent whole lessons shooting nervous glances at them as if they were a flock of angry plovers about to attack. After two weeks our classroom walls had become so splattered with words it looked like a massive bomb had exploded in a library.

It was on the Friday before Sally Nofke's party that Miss Tarango unrolled a big poster written in swirling letters and gold leaf and taped it to the front of the teacher's desk. It was a poem called 'Desiderata', which Miss told us meant 'Things to be desired'. I thought of the party on Saturday night. I knew what I desired.

I liked the poem. We even listened to it on CD. Mostly it gave a lot of advice like how you should 'be yourself' and 'listen to others' and that kind of stuff. But some parts made me think about things in my own life. Bits like 'avoid loud and aggressive persons' who the writer reckoned were 'vexations to the spirit' (which Razza translated as 'pains in the arse'). This reminded me a lot of Barry Bagsley. It also said you shouldn't compare yourself to others or you might become bitter, which made me think of my little sister Prue and how she's a near-genius and how I'm... well... a sort of far-off-galaxy genius.

What I really liked, though, was the bit near the end that reckoned I was 'a child of the universe' and that 'no less than the trees and the stars, I had a right to be here'. I was kind of hoping Barry Bagsley and his mates would take note of that. Somehow I didn't fancy my chances.

But it was the next line that really stuck with me – the one that ended by saying, no doubt the universe was 'unfolding as it should'. I began to wonder whether that could be true. And that started me thinking about Kelly Faulkner and how I thought I'd never get the chance to speak to her since she was just so perfect, but then just because I'd seen a primary kid being bullied and tried to help him and that kid ended up being Kelly Faulkner's little brother, Kelly came to thank me and so I did get to speak to her and now, because of all that, Kelly had invited Razza and me to her friend's party and I'd be seeing her again tomorrow night.

The more I looked at it, the more convinced I became that all the time I'd been worried that my life had about as much direction as a dragster with a blow-out, my universe had actually been 'unfolding as it should'.

I still had that amazing thought in my head on Saturday night as Razza and I jumped into the back seat of his mum's car and we set off for Sally Nofke's party.

Little did I know, but by the time the party was over, my universe wouldn't be 'unfolding' any more. It would be falling apart at the seams.

Track 2:
Dead Toad
Society Blues

I'm lyin' on the road, I got no place to go
I'm beaten and I'm broken and bust
I'm battered to the ground, splattered all around
Cannot move a muscle, but must
Everything feels broken – man you must be jokin'
To say you'd rather burn out than rust

Chorus
I got the Dead Toad Society, Dead Toad Society,
Dead Toad Society blues!
I got the Dead Toad Society, the deadliest variety of,
The Dead Toad Society blues!

From The Dugongs: *Returned & Remastered*
Music & lyrics: W. Mangan and R. Leseur

7.
So Fully Empty

We were dropped off at Sally's house just after seven.

"Time to par-taaaay!" Razza said, jabbing the doorbell and breaking into a jerky robotic dance. I was about to say something about the 'old laid-back approach' when the door clicked open and a girl appeared.

"Hi," she said, smiling and pushing her long dark hair back behind her ears. "I'm Sally. You must be Ishmael and Orazio?"

Her voice was warm and kind of husky, like it was frayed around the edges. For some reason it made me think of coffee, which I thought was strange because

I don't like coffee. I was pretty sure that I was going to like Sally Nofke though – and I was certain I wasn't the only one with that thought.

"Hi. He's Ishmael. I'm Orazio, but most people call me Razza."

"Well, glad you guys could make it. Come on in."

We moved inside and Razza handed over a present.

"Happy birthday – from both of us."

"Oh, you really didn't have to bring anything – but that's lovely. Thank you."

"Hope you like chocolates," Razza said.

"With a passion," Sally said, and her dark eyes sparkled.

"Great. We were thinking of a CD but didn't know what you were into. I reckoned the new one by Tranz Phat would have been wicked."

"Wow, they rock. I love their stuff."

"Yeah? Cool! Same here," Razza said.

"I really like 'Ninja love'."

"Same here!" Razza said again. "What an awesome drum beat, eh. Man, I *knew* we shoulda got you that CD."

Razza and Sally grinned at each other briefly before Sally's eyes dropped quickly to the chocolates. "But no, these are great, too. I'll just have to hide them from my little brother and sister, otherwise they'll disappear for sure."

"Hey, you guys made it."

I turned towards the voice. It was Kelly Faulkner. Later I would remember other things about her, like how her yellow T-shirt just reached to the top of her jeans and how her belt buckle locked together in the form of butterfly wings, and I would even notice the embroidery around her back pockets and her multi-coloured shoes, but at that moment all I could see were pale ice-blue eyes, the soft curve of a smile and a face that seemed to shine.

"Hi," I said, quickly finding myself at the outer reaches of my conversational skills, "... Ah... you remember Razza."

"Of course," Kelly said. "How could I forget the famous Razzman?" Then she spoke behind her hand to Sally. "I really shouldn't be telling you this, Sal, but the goss on the street is that this guy is a bit of a superhero in disguise."

"Really?" Sally said, looking Razz up and down and pretending to be impressed.

"Yep, I heard it right from the sidekick's mouth," Kelly said, nodding towards me.

"Are you *really* a superhero?" Sally asked with a smile.

"Please, please," Razza said, holding up his hands and shaking his head, "everyone just says that... because it's true."

Both girls rolled their eyes and laughed. Unfortunately it was cut short by the chiming of the doorbell.

"That'd have to be Jess – everyone else is here."

Sally opened the door and was quickly swamped by squeals of "Happy Birthday!" and smothered in an embrace. Then the new arrival grabbed Sally's arm, dragged her across the room towards us and bounced in beside Kelly. Razza seemed transfixed by the fact that not *all* of her stopped bouncing at the same time.

"Hey, Kel. You look *so* great."

"Thanks – you too. New outfit?" The new girl wore a short frilly white skirt that hugged her hips like it was going in for a low tackle and a plunging top that seemed to be fighting a desperate rearguard action to keep everything in.

"Yeah, got it from Catwalk. It was like so on sale."

"Great. Anyway… Jess, this is Ishmael… and this is Razza."

It wasn't hard to read Razza's mind as we exchanged hellos and he ran his eyes over Jess. Any second I expected the word "Hot!" to appear in big sizzling letters on his forehead.

"Hey, Jess, check out the scrummy chockies the guys gave me."

"Cool! Be no good for me though," Jess said, patting a flat, tanned section of bare midriff. "I have to watch my figure."

"Well, if you ever want a break," Razza said, "I'd be happy to watch it for you."

Jess opened her mouth then squealed with delight, "That – is – *so* – funny! I think I'd better watch you," she said, placing her hand on Razza's arm.

The two other girls exchanged a quick look and Kelly jumped in with, "Well, Sal's got no worries about putting on weight, not with all the tennis and football she does."

Razza's face lit up. "You play *football*?"

"A bit."

"A bit! She's only captain of the school team as well

as her local club team *and* she's reserve for the State side."

Razza looked impressed. "Cool!" he said.

Sally blushed a little. "Well, my dad grew up in England. He's a mad keen Liverpool supporter – me too, actually, especially since Harry Kewell used to be in the team."

"Yeah... they're not bad... for an *English* team," Razz said knowingly, "but if you want a *real* team, you have to go to Italy – AC Milan, mate, now *that's* a real football club."

"AC Milan? AC Milan? Now let me think," Sally said, smirking and rubbing her chin, "would *that* be the same AC Milan that was *thrashed* in the final of the 2005 UEFA Champions League by... Ummmmm, let me see... Who *was* it now? It's on the tip of my tongue... Oh, I remember... That's right... *Liverpool.*"

"Thrashed? What d'ya mean, thrashed? It was a three-all draw, for crying out loud! You just won because of a stupid penalty shoot-out and some freaky saves. Everyone knows we were robbed!"

"Yes... Of *course* you were," Sally crooned before swaying from side to side and chanting softly, "Liiiiiiv-er-pool! Liiiiiiv-er-pool!"

Razza covered his ears. "No, don't remind me. The nightmare returns! Aaaaaarrrrrhhhh!"

Sally patted Razza on the shoulder. "There, there, there. It's all right. Don't cry. There's always next year – *if* you make it."

We were all having a laugh at Razza's expense when Jess broke in. "Hey Sal, I almost forgot to give you your present. Here you go. Happy birthday!" she said, hugging Sally again and slipping in between her and Razza. "Hope you haven't got it already. It's a Tiffany Jackson CD."

"Tiffany Jackson?"

Jess turned towards Razz. "Yeah, you like her?"

Razza grimaced a little. "Well… 'like' is a very strong word."

"I think she's way cool – she's like fully hot."

"Yeah, she's *hot*… but…"

"Hey Jess, thanks a lot. We'll put it on later. It'll be great to dance to."

"Cool! It's got all her greatest hits on it."

Beside me Razza mumbled something about it being a "blank CD" then, which luckily Jess didn't catch. Sally, on the other hand, seemed to be biting her top lip and trying not to look at Kelly.

"Here you all are." A boy had just come in from the next room and joined the circle, moving in beside Kelly. He looked like an apprentice Brad Pitt.

"Hi, I'm Brad," he said, thrusting his hand out towards me. Why wasn't I surprised? Razza and I both introduced ourselves and shook hands. "Hey, I hear you guys go to St Daniel's. Your Firsts really gave it to us last year in the rugby – only game we lost all season."

"So you're from Churchill Grammar, then," Razz said. "Well, we'll talk to you now, but after the party we'll have to kill you. Nothing personal – it's school policy."

Brad laughed and showed his perfect teeth. "Fair enough," he said.

"Just wait till next year when *you're* in the Firsts, Brad," Jess said. "They'll be totally unbeatable."

"*If* I make the team, you mean – my parents reckon I have to do well in all my subjects this year or I can forget about even trying out."

"You'll be fine," Sally said.

"Maybe, but we're not all geniuses like you, Sal. Some of us get other letters on our reports besides As."

"Genius?" Sally said with an embarrassed laugh. "I don't think so."

"No? Then I guess that Outstanding Achievement certificate you got in the National Maths Competition was just a fluke."

"He's right, Sal. You're a real brain. You're so going to be top of the school when we graduate."

Sally's cheeks and neck turned blotchy red. "Can we talk about something else?" she said, dropping her head and letting her hair fall around her face.

"Hey, stop embarrassing her," Kelly said, shooting a cold look at Brad. "Sally works hard and deserves everything she gets."

"Sorry, Sal," Brad said. "Don't worry about me. I'm just jealous, that's all. Anyway, to change the subject, what I actually came out here to tell you all in the first place was that food's being served out on the deck and if you're not careful you'll miss out."

"Food? Boy, I could do with some of that," Jess said, shaking her head. "Before I left home I was feeling like… hungry… but… *not*, you know what I mean? Anyway, Mum's like, 'You *have* to eat something', and I'm like, 'No, I so don't', and she's like, 'You're wasting away', and I'm like, '*What*ever', and then she goes like fully psycho and I'm like, 'Excuse me?' *Then* in the car coming over it was sooo embarrassing 'cause Mum's so like totally giving me the silent treatment and I'm like, 'Well if she's not talking, I'm not talking', but then my tummy got an attack of the rumbles and it's going like, 'Grrrrrrrrrr', so loudly 'cause, yeah… It's so like… you know… so fully… so fully empty!"

Jess just stood there holding her stomach and smiling at everyone with her mouth wide open until Razza said, "So… let's like… eat!"

As I moved off with the others I was pretty excited about the night ahead – or at least I was, until in front of me I saw Brad slip his hand into Kelly's and smile down at her. I held my breath. I was still holding it when Kelly smiled back and entwined her fingers with his.

Jess was absolutely right. Sometimes you can just feel like… you know… so fully empty.

8.
The Dung Beetle in the Ecosystem of Love

"Hey, what's up with you, man?"

It was an hour or so later. We'd been introduced around, met Sally's family, had some food out on the back deck and spent time in the house with Sally and her friends listening to music and dancing. Now while the others were setting up a karaoke machine inside, I was getting some fresh air beside the pool. I looked up as Razza joined me.

"What do you mean?"

"Well, mate," Razza said, "I gotta tell you, you're not exactly being the life of the party, you know."

I suppose he had a point. I was *trying* to join in and

have fun, although as a dancer I'd make an excellent shop dummy and I had a strong feeling that the title of King of Karaoke wouldn't be coming my way any time soon. It's just that whenever I saw Kelly with Brad I felt like I was free falling with my heart wedged somewhere in my throat.

"I'm fine."

"You reckon? Well, what are you moping around out here for, man? I'm telling you, if you want to win Kelly tonight you're gonna have to lift your game."

"Win Kelly? You're kidding, aren't you? Didn't you meet Brad – *Teen Magazine*'s Super Spunk of the Year?"

"Ah, so that's it. A little competition and you're chucking in the towel."

"Yep, that's the plan."

"You're mad. Listen, I've seen this sort of thing loads of times. It's always the same. It goes like this. There's this dorky funny sort of dude – that's you – and he meets this really cute chick – that's Kelly – so naturally he gets the terminal hots for her, only then he finds out she's already got this meathead of a boyfriend – that's Brad. Anyway, a lot of wacky things happen but eventually the really cute chick realises her boyfriend is a dirt bag and that the dorky dude is a nice guy and she falls for him and they end up getting hot and heavy together. End of story."

"Razz, you've only seen that loads of times because it's the plot of every American teen movie ever made."

"Maybe, but Hollywood wouldn't lie, would they?"

"Well anyway, I think there might be a *tiny* flaw in your theory. Have you noticed that Brad doesn't happen to be a 'meathead' or a 'dirt bag'? Have you noticed that he's actually a nice guy and pretty smart as well? Have you noticed how everyone likes him? Geez, even *I* like him, and I *hate* the guy."

"They're just details," Razz said, waving me away. "Look, it's like my football coach says – what you gotta do is find where you have the 'competitive edge' over your opposition and then exploit that to your advantage."

"Right, well let's see. What have we discovered about Brad and me in the course of the evening? Well, we both play rugby, but unfortunately he plays A grade and I play in a team so far down the alphabet that you'd have to watch three years of *Sesame Street* just to recognise the letter."

"Look, if you're going to…"

"No, wait… there's more. He's good-looking, well built, fit and a champion athlete and I'm… *not*; he's got confidence, charisma and personality and… hey, what do you know, I *don't*. So tell me, Razz, where precisely do you think my 'competitive edge' lies?"

"Hmmmm… well," Razza said thoughtfully, "are you handy with a rocket launcher at all?"

"Exactly."

"Man, you need to chill out. You're reading way too much into this Kelly and Brad thing, anyway. Sure he's sort of *with* her tonight and they're dancing together a bit and there might be some handies every now and then, but she's not all over him like a rash, is she? So what I reckon is, he digs her much more than she digs him. I mean, you gotta admit, dude, it's hardly been a grope-a-thon or duelling tongues, has it?"

I didn't know whether Razz was making sense or I just desperately wanted to believe him. "No, I suppose not."

"Right – so you gotta snap out of it, man, and let Kelly see what she's missing out on. And just remember, she invited you to this party and she wouldn't have done that if she didn't like you, okay?"

"I guess."

I looked across to the house where Sally and Jess were talking excitedly over a pile of CDs.

"Anyway, what about you? You seem to be making quite an impression tonight."

"Yeah, I'm gonna see if I can get Jess's number later. Man, she's so hot, she's white. She's white hot."

"Jess? What about Sally?"

Razza gazed over into the house and for a rare moment went quiet. "Yeah… Sally's really cool… She's great… but I don't think she's my type."

"Not your type? What are you talking about, not your type? You guys like the same music, you're both into football and you've both got the same warped sense of humour. I mean, I know Jess is well… Jess is *incredible*, but Sally's… she's something else."

"I know all that… but you heard what they said. She's a brainiac, mate. She's a chick version of Prindabel."

"Razz, Prindabel never looked *anything* like that."

"Yeah, all right… but why would the future top student of Lourdes College want to hang out with me? She got an Outstanding Achievement certificate in the

National Maths Competition, dude. You know what I got – a sympathy card. Don't laugh, it's true. 'Dear Mr Zorzotto, please accept our deepest condolences on the tragic loss of your brain.'"

"Get out of here – you're not dumb. Do you think you could come up with all those jokes if you were dumb? You've got brains all right, plenty of them."

"Really? Gee, do you think you could explain that to my teachers, because according to my report cards, there seems to be some confusion." Razza took a deep breath. "Look, all I'm saying is, I know my limits and Sally's way too brainy to want anything to do with me."

This didn't sound like the Razza I knew.

"So let me get this straight. It's all right for you to give up just because Sally gets some stupid certificate, but when *I* find out Kelly is going with Mr Perfect I'm not allowed to wave the old white flag."

"It's not the same."

"Seems like it to me."

"No, it's not. You see, we're different. For you it's Kelly Faulkner or no one. You're a sucker for all that love stuff. But me, I'm willing to accept defeat, cut my losses and give someone else a chance to enjoy the obvious pleasure of my company."

"Right, and of course I suppose it makes it easier to cut your losses when that someone else just happens to have some sizeable *assets* of her own?"

Razza raised an eyebrow at me. "What are you getting at?"

"I was just wondering how much Jess's 'white-hot bod' might have influenced your decision."

Razza's mouth dropped open. "What... Are you seriously suggesting that that's all I care about? Do you really think that just because some chick has the face of a centrefold goddess and the body of a lingerie model and is not afraid to show it, that *somehow* that's important to me?" He looked around wildly as if the world had turned against him. "Are... Are you accusing me of being... *shallow*?"

"I just wondered..."

"Well... maybe I am a *little* shallow," Razza said with a quick smile, then pointed a finger at me. "But it's not like *you* think. It's different. It's a... a... *deep* kind of shallow."

"What!"

"You heard me – a deep kind of shallow. Yeah, that's

right, just imagine if every guy was like you and thought stuff like personality, brains and being nice were more important than a to-die-for bod and a kick-ass face. I'm telling you, man, it would be chaos."

I shook my head in disbelief, but Razza was only just warming to his task.

"Yeah, if every guy was like you, just imagine all the really hot chicks who'd be lonely and abandoned. But because of me, and guys like me, hot chicks can rest easy knowing that we're there to take care of them. Now, don't you feel ashamed of yourself? Do you see now how selfish and narrow-minded you really are?"

"Yes, I get it now. Looks like I had you all wrong. You're kind of like… providing an important community service for hot chicks, is that it?"

Razza clicked his fingers as a crazy fire started to burn in his eyes. "Yeah, you got it exactly, man – an essential community service. Like a doctor… or, or… a social worker. Yeah, that's it. That's what I am. I'm a social worker for love. I'm doing my bit, man. I'm… part of the web of love!"

"Part of the *what*?"

"Part of the web of love – you know, just like that

web of life thing that Hackworth's always going on about in science – all that delicate balance of the ecosystem crap where all the animals and birds and plants are sort of linked together with creepy stuff like grubs and dung beetles and even those bacteria dudes in the soil."

"Right. So don't tell me, let me guess. You'd be the dung beetle in the ecosystem of love, would you?"

"Well you may laugh, Leseur, but I'll *tell* you what I am," he said as his eyes darted about searching for inspiration. "I'm… I'm…" Then he stopped and his eyes glowed with wonder at the night sky. "I'm a child of the universe," he said grandly, raising his arms into the air, "no less than the fleas and cigars – I have a *right* to be here!"

I studied Razza closely but still couldn't work out whether he was being serious or just trying to be funny. It was also difficult to decide which of those two possibilities I found more disturbing.

9.
Eeeeeeeeeeeuuuu uuwwwwwww!

I survived the karaoke by playing a small but vital role as one of the back-up singers in various performances including an enthusiastic but melodically challenged version of 'We are the champions'.

The real highlights, though, were Kelly and Sally doing a medley from *Grease* that was better than the original, Jess doing a Tiffany Jackson song with dance moves that made you completely forget that her voice sounded like someone had reversed a steamroller over a chihuahua, and Razza bringing the house down with a truly scary imitation of Elvis with 'All shook up'. But what really had me cheering on the inside was the discovery that Brad was definitely no rock god and, like me, was happy to restrict himself to backing vocals.

The evening was certainly looking up. That is to say it was until someone said, "Hey, how about a swim?"

This is what I'd been dreading. I could just see myself stranded in my trunks beside alpha male Brad and looking like the unbackable favourite in the Mr Puny-verse competition. I decided my only hope was to get changed fast and submerge myself in the relative safety of the pool. So, while most of the others were still chatting away or getting themselves organised, I grabbed my gear and slipped into the nearest bathroom.

By the time I made it to the pool there were only two other people in the water – a guy and a girl up the deep end who seemed much more interested in each other than me. I threw my towel over a chair and dived in. Not long after, Brad came out and started talking to the couple at the far end of the pool. It gave me a chance to check out his muscles – I guess he had a few here and there. Who was I kidding? Brad had muscles where I didn't even have a here and there. I inspected my own tanned and bulging arms in the pale light. They looked like two bent fluorescent tubes. I sank down to my neck in the water.

Pretty soon a couple of girls joined me in the shallow end and started talking quietly together. I paddled about and waited for Razza.

A little while later Sally's baby sister Sophie wandered out struggling with a big plastic bottle of orange cordial. She looked around before coming over to the edge of the pool. "It don't open," she said, thrusting it towards me. "You do it?"

I took it from her and loosened the top. "There you go," I said as I handed it back. Sophie wrapped her little fingers eagerly around the bottle but it slipped from her grasp and torpedoed into the water. For a second she stood there with her mouth gaping, then she burst into tears and ran back inside. The girls beside me turned briefly to see what the disturbance was, but by then it was all over.

With only the light coming from the house to work by, I started feeling around for the bottle with my feet. I was busy peering into the shadowy depths when I stepped forward and felt my foot land on something that started off firm but then popped and squashed flat under my weight.

At that exact moment Sally called from the back

deck, "Hey, do you guys want some light down there?" and suddenly the water around me lit up like a bright blue screen. More people spilled out from the house. Two boys dive-bombed into the deep end. I looked up at Sally and smiled, but for some reason she didn't smile back. And neither did the red-haired girl beside her – the one who was screwing up her face and pointing at me in horror.

I looked down at myself. At first I thought their reaction was because the underwater pool lights had turned my already pale body into a frightening replica of Gollum from *Lord of the Rings*. But then I saw it. A sinister yellowy-green cloud was spilling out from between my legs and billowing towards the surface. *It's just the cordial*, I thought. My eyes flicked back to the deck. Sally looked ill. The red-haired girl was opening her mouth. "No… no… It's just…' But that was as far as I got. The red-haired girl's face shrivelled up as if she was being force-fed a lemon, and then she let out a loud and extended "Eeeeeeeeeeeeeuuuuuuwwwwww!"

Instantly, around twenty pairs of eyes shot to the deck and then traced the line of the pointing finger back to the pool like they were tracking a ricocheting bullet. Twenty pairs of eyes came to rest on my groin. Two of those pairs of eyes belonged to the girls beside me who stood mesmerised as a stain of yellowy-green water snaked out from my trunks and began to curl around their waists. We all looked up at the same time. Our eyes met. "No… no… It's just…" But that was as far as I got before they showed their tonsils and unleashed upon the world the shrillest, the most brain-piercing sound ever produced by human vocal chords. If only the *Guinness Book of Records* people could have been there to witness it. It was the sound of the universe unravelling. It was accompanied by a mad blur of hands churning up the water like a thousand outboard motors and a hysterical mass evacuation that would have been right at home in *Jaws*.

When the panic finally settled I was left standing alone in a choppy pool surrounded by a yellowy-green smudge and towered over by a circle of appalled faces.

Just when you think it's safe to go back in the water (Daaaaaa-dum… daaaaaa-dum… da-dum-da-dum-da-dum-da-dum-da-dum), Ishmael Leseur's Syndrome grabs you with its razor-sharp teeth.

10.
The Human Rip

"You know, maybe it's just me, but if I was desperate to win on to some chick, I really don't think pissing in her best friend's pool would be that high up on my to-do list."

"It. Was. *Cordial.*"

I grated out the words between clenched teeth as I imagined myself inflicting on Razza a variety of slow and excruciating forms of torture.

He looked at me through narrowing eyes. "Cordial? Sure. *Originally.*"

It was Monday morning, and we were waiting for Miss Tarango to arrive for English. I was sick of trying to explain away what Razza kept referring to as the Pool Piddle Affair or Piss-in-the-Watergate. I'd been through it enough on Saturday night, and the memory of those horrified faces burning down on me like spotlights was scorched permanently into my brain.

Of course I'd tried to explain. I told them about Sophie and the cordial bottle. But all they did was nod, smile weakly and exchange knowing glances. Sally, Kelly and Razza supported me, but I could tell the others weren't convinced. I wasn't helped much by the fact that Sophie, who obviously thought she was being accused of some horrendous crime, clammed up and refused to confirm my story. Not only that, but the cordial bottle seemed to have vanished and, strangely enough, no one was keen on leaping into the pool to help me search for it. I felt surrounded by some kind of force field that repelled anyone who got too close. I couldn't really blame them, I suppose. After all, they had just witnessed first-hand the horrors of Ishmael Leseur's Syndrome and were probably petrified that it might be contagious.

"*You* believe me, don't you, Razz? I mean... *really?*"

He stopped twirling his pen and looked at me.

"Yeah… Yeah, I guess I do. You're just not the *Star Trek* commander type, are you?"

"What's that supposed to mean?"

"You know," Razz said with a smile, "you're not the kind of dude who boldly *goes* where no man has *gone* before."

I smiled too. I didn't think I'd be doing that for a while. Razza rolled his pen through his fingers then flicked it up so that it twirled like a helicopter rotor blade on his knuckles before sliding neatly back into his grasp.

"Hey Razz… look… Sorry about Jess and everything."

Unfortunately, at the party poor old Razz had suffered badly from guilt by association, and Jess, who up to the incident in the pool had been showing a lot of interest, suddenly kept her distance. Just by being my friend and sticking with me, Razz had been stained as well – and the stain was yellowy-green. By the time we left, Jess had become very friendly with a mate of Brad's from Churchill Grammar.

"Nah, forget it. Look at it this way – at least you saved me from Tiffany Jackson. Anyway, don't forget that our real problem is how to get you and Kelly together."

I'll just let you imagine the expression on my face. "Do you have these fits often? Me and Kelly? Razz, there is no me and Kelly. It's over – surely even *you* can see that? I don't think I've exactly improved my chances against Brad, do you? I mean, in a battle to the death between Captain America and Urine Boy, you're hardly going to put your money on me, are you?"

"I don't know – judging by Saturday night's effort, I'd say you'd probably piss it in." Razza threw back his head and laughed at his own joke. "Now *that's* gold," he said, "… or possibly yellow."

I buried my head in my hands.

"Look, dude, you're worrying way too much about the pool bit. That's just one of those wacky things I told you would happen before you two finally get it on."

"Wacky? You think being labelled a serial pool wetter is wacky?"

"Yeah," Razza said looking surprised, "don't you?"

"No… no, I don't. And do you know why? Because I'm what is generally referred to as 'normal' and you're what's commonly known as 'a complete nutter'. You are. You're mad, Razz. Kelly and I won't 'get it on'. It'll never happen. It's over."

"No way. It's not over till the fat chick sings."

I couldn't believe it. It was like talking to a brick wall, only brick walls don't argue back and they don't grin stupidly at you as if *you're* the one with your head filled with cement.

"Razz, she's sung already, all right. She's... she's packed up and gone home, and by now she's probably six weeks into her weight-loss programme at Jenny Craig's and already 40 kilos lighter. Read my lips – *it's over*. I've got no hope with Kelly Faulkner. I got nothin'."

"Wrong, wrong, wrong," Razza said with a smug smile. "You got *me*."

"Hey, that's right! How could I forget? I've got you – the social worker for love. I feel a lot better now. Mind if I borrow your mobile? I think I'll invite Kelly over for a sleepover this weekend."

"Awesome! Hold on – would your folks be cool with that?"

I bent forward until my forehead thudded on the desk. I was exhausted. It was useless trying to fight Razza. It was like being caught in a giant rip at the beach. You could struggle against it all you like, but you'd just end up draining all your energy and drowning. They reckon the trick is to relax and let the rip take you out to sea and then, when it weakens, all you have to do is signal for the lifeguards or drift down a bit and ride the waves back to the shore.

Well, here I was, sitting right beside the Human Rip. I realised that if I kept struggling against him he'd eventually suck every last ounce of strength from me and I'd end up agreeing to anything just to shut him up. That's when I decided to apply the Surf Safety approach – just go along with Razza, pretend to let him carry me away with his mad ideas for a while. I figured he'd run out of steam eventually and then I'd simply paddle calmly back to reality.

It really did seem like a good plan, and I was sure that those lifeguards and beach-safety-expert people would be pleased. But still… I'd often wondered. What if the rip you get caught in is *really* strong? What if it carries you so far out that you can't touch the bottom and the waves are huge and you can't even see the beach any more? What if you start to cramp up before the lifeguards arrive? And what if there are sharks out there waiting for you?

"Man, you got nothing to worry about," I heard

Razza say. "It's cool. Leave it with me. I'm gonna come up with a *wicked* plan!"

I could feel the current tugging at my legs and the sand slipping from under my feet. I hoped the lifeguards were paying attention. I lifted my head off the desk and turned to Razza. He was tapping both temples rapidly with his fingers as if he was trying to stimulate his brain into action and his eyes were bouncing around like dodgem cars.

That's when the awful reality hit me. I was about to let myself be swept away by Orazio Zorzotto, and there was no way in the world we were swimming between the flags.

11.
Me and You and Shaky Bill

A couple of weeks went by and Razza hadn't said any more about his 'wicked plan', so I was beginning to think that maybe the Human Rip was already dead in the water. The sea can fool you, though – just when everything appears calm, conditions can turn treacherous.

One day Miss Tarango bustled in, chirped out a cheery, "Morning all!", laid her books on the teacher's desk and moved to the front of the class where she waited for silence. Then she smiled and breathed in deeply. Her voice, when it came, was soft and slow like melted chocolate. "*How do I love thee?*" she said, holding her arms wide. "*Let me count the ways.*"

A murmur washed around the room carrying with it stray comments and laughter.

Miss Tarango took no notice. "*I love thee to the depth and breadth and height my soul can reach.*"

She looked to the back of the room where Barry Bagsley and his mates were sprawled.

"*I love thee to the level of every day's most quiet need, by sun and candlelight.*"

She passed her eyes around the middle of the class where Scobie, Razza and I were seated. "*I love thee freely as men strive for Right; I love thee purely as they turn from praise.*"

She looked down at the boys in front of her, including Bill Kingsley and Ignatius Prindabel. "*I love thee with the passion put to use in my old griefs, and with my childhood's faith.*"

Then her eyes swept all around the room and she smiled so that her dimples appeared like two tiny kisses on her cheeks. "*I love thee,*" she said, as she crossed her hands over her heart, "*with all the breath... smiles... tears... of all my life.*"

For a moment I imagined Kelly Faulkner saying those words to me, and my insides felt like they were melting and dripping away like wax. When Miss finished, nobody spoke. I don't think anyone really wanted her to stop.

"Boys," she said finally, "today we are immersing ourselves in Love. What I have recited to you just now were some lines from a sonnet by Elizabeth Barrett Browning. This poem and others, including a selection of Shakespeare's love sonnets, are on this handout."

Sheets of paper dipped and dived about the room.

"Now, let's see," Miss Tarango said as her eyes glided around the class. "Ah... yes, the very man... Ignatius..."

At the mention of his name Prindabel, who'd been clutching his sheet and glaring at it as if it were a death threat, jerked back in horror.

"You'll be able to tell me, Ignatius. What do all the poems on the handout have in common?"

Prindabel stared back as if he'd been accused of murder. Slowly he turned to the sheet in his hands. He squinted at it like he was translating ancient hieroglyphics, scratched his pointy nose, then looked up gingerly and muttered, "Is it... that they all have... fourteen lines, Miss?"

Beside me Razza snorted loudly, slapped his

forehead, rolled his eyes and let his head fall with a loud clunk on to the back of his chair.

"Precisely, Ignatius!" Miss Tarango said.

Prindabel gaped at her as if he'd just escaped a firing squad but had no idea how.

At the same time, Razza catapulted himself forward on his chair. "You're *joking*, Miss. You mean he was *right*?"

"Absolutely, Orazio. All sonnets have fourteen lines. Some, depending on their rhyming scheme, can be divided into a section of eight lines called an octave plus a section of six lines called a sestet. Other sonnets, like the Shakespearean ones, have three quatrains or four-line sections with a final rhyming couplet making up the fourteen. You should also be able to find five beats to each line, so I suppose you could say that there's a fair bit of *maths* in these poems."

Prindabel immediately snaffled up his pen and began ticking, counting, underlining and marking off sections of verse. As he did so, he chewed on his bottom lip and nodded deliberately. Finally a crooked smile cut across his face. For the first time in his life, poetry seemed to be speaking to Ignatius Prindabel.

"Okay, boys, let's start off with Shakespeare's

Sonnet 18 – 'Shall I compare thee to a summer's day?' Now listen carefully as I read it through, and then go over it yourselves a few times before we discuss it."

We listened again to Miss Tarango's warm and silky voice before turning reluctantly to the tangle of cold, dark words on the page. After a while Miss said, "Right, now. Let's have a look at the first quatrain and see what we can make of it:

> *Shall I compare thee to a summer's day?*
> *Thou art more lovely and more temperate:*
> *Rough winds do shake the darling buds of May,*
> *And summer's lease hath all too short a date.*

Any takers?"

James Scobie stretched his mouth to the left and to the right, then raised his hand. Miss Tarango waited to see if there would be other volunteers. Suddenly Razza sat bolt upright beside me.

"Wick-*ed*!" he said, grinning madly. "I *get* it, Miss. I get it. Man, I can dig this Shakespeare dude!"

"Well, that's wonderful, Orazio," Miss said, raising her eyebrows. "Let's hear it then."

"Well, he's obviously writing about some chick, see... and he's saying how she's like a summer's day only better. Well... summer's *hot*, right? So I reckon old Shakey's trying to win some chick by telling her how hot she is. So like, they're probably at a party or something and I think there's a big storm or whatever – that's the bit about the *rough winds* shaking the *buds* – and anyway, the chick's had enough and wants to go home early but Shakey's hanging out for some more action, right – see that's when he whinges about it being *all too short a date*, 'cause he wants her to stick around a bit longer so he can maybe score *another* date with her. Yeah, so that's basically it – it's just all about trying to win some hot chick. Am I right or am I right, Miss?"

Miss Tarango seemed to have gone a little pale. "Orazio," she said, shaking her head, "you never cease to amaze me. We might have to look just a *little* more closely at some of those ideas, but you are certainly on the right track when you say that Shakespeare is expressing his love and admiration towards the subject of the poem. Love sonnets were an extremely popular form back then."

"Yeah, but chicks in Shakespeare's day didn't really go for this schmaltzy stuff did they, Miss?"

"Well, if you are asking me, Orazio, if I think *young women* in Shakespeare's time would have *appreciated* being complimented and praised with such *grace, beauty* and *eloquence* – then I'd have to say I'm sure they did; as I'm equally certain would many young women today."

Razza's eyes expanded alarmingly. "*Really*, Miss? You mean you reckon chi... *young women* today would be stoked if guys wrote them poetry?"

"Well, I can't speak for all the sisters, Orazio, but I'd be surprised if there were very many young women today who *didn't* think that receiving a poem as a form of admiration wouldn't beat the *hell* out of being *whistled, shouted, ogled* or *grunted* at."

The colour certainly seemed to have come back to Miss Tarango's cheeks. She glanced quickly around the room. "Well... anyway... We seem to have digressed a little. Let's get back to Sonnet 18, shall we?"

I don't really remember that much about the rest of the lesson, I'm afraid. I do, however, recall Razza turning to me with some kind of madness dancing in his eyes and whispering, "Chicks are hot for poetry... *Awesome!*"

When the bell finally sounded and the class began

to pour from the room, Razza grabbed my arm. "We're *in*, dude! We are so *sweet*!"

"Razz, what are you talking about now?"

"Weren't you paying attention? Didn't you hear what Miss T said? Chicks dig poetry – so that's *it*!"

"That's *what*?"

Razza pulled at his hair. "You know, sometimes I wonder why I bother. That's the *plan*, dude. That's how you and Kelly Faulkner are going to get together. You write her a love poem, dude, just like the Shakey man!"

The bottom fell away beneath my feet and the beach became a distant memory. I tried not to struggle too much. I just wanted to keep my head above water.

"Razz, you know… I'm thinking… maybe that's not such a great idea."

"What do you mean? It rocks. Miss is right. Chicks go for that sloppy stuff."

"Yeah… but I just can't… You know… send Kelly Faulkner a poem out of the blue."

"Sure you can. Why not? Look, you weren't there, but the other night, when I was rapping with our mate Brad and crapping on to him about school and having to do Shakespeare, he reckoned he was glad it was me and not him, but *Kelly* said she loved that kind of stuff. Don'tcha see? This is it. This is your competitive edge. It's like you're one of the X-men and your special mutant power is poetry. This is how you beat your evil nemesis Brad the Bad."

"Razz, how can poetry be my 'special mutant power' when I've never even written a poem before?"

"A mere technicality," Razz said, waving me away with his hand. "The thing is, you can write – remember how Miss went ga-ga over that diary thing you put together last year? And poetry's easy as. Just chuck in a few *thees* and *thous*, a couple of rhymes, a few beating hearts and some 'my love is this, my love is that' bull and Kelly Faulkner will be salivating all over you like you were a double quarter pounder with the works."

"I doubt if it's that simple."

"Course it is. Man, between the three of us, it'll be sweet!"

"Three of us? What three of us?"

"Me and you and Shakey Bill. Awesome! Dude, it's the Dream Team. How can we fail?"

At that, Razza leaped up and stuffed his books into his desk. "Gotta bolt – football meeting." He disappeared out the door and left me alone in a sea of empty desks.

How could we fail? I asked myself, sensing dark shapes circling around me.

Let me count the ways.

Track 3: Each and Every Line

I'm not much at talking
But I'll tell you what I'll do
I'll lock myself away till I
Can find the words for you

Chorus
Stay still so I can catch you
Stay close I'll make you mine
Say yes and I will weave you
Into each and every line.

From The Dugongs: *Returned & Remastered*
Music & lyrics: R. Leseur

12.
The Inaugural
St Daniel's College
Crap-a-thon

For the next few days Razz hassled me non-stop about the poem, wanting to know if I'd started on it, how it was coming along and when it'd be finished. I tried to fob him off by saying vague things like, "not too bad", "it's getting there", "pretty soon", and "I'm working on it". But as far as I was concerned, my special mutant super power was never going to see the light of day.

Things were looking good too. By the end of the first term the Human Rip appeared to have run out of steam. The interrogations about the poem had dwindled to nothing, and as the holidays arrived I imagined myself catching a wave all the way back to the safety of the beach.

Pity about those dumpers, though.

Everything started to go pear-shaped soon after the break, when Scobie called a surprise debating meeting. The season didn't officially start until the second term, but he was eager to get things rolling early. I guess he wanted to improve on last year's effort, when thanks mainly to his brilliance and a lucky topic about sci-fi, which just happened to be Bill's special subject, we made it all the way to the semi-finals.

As for my part in our success… Well, thankfully I've managed to suppress most of those memories, so if you're curious you will have to borrow last year's diary. Be warned though, it contains graphic descriptions of Ishmael Leseur's Syndrome that might offend some readers.

On the day of the meeting, Bill Kingsley, Ignatius Prindabel, James Scobie and I sat around a small cluster of desks that we'd pushed together in our form room. Scobie threw another look at the clock on the wall and then at me. "He knew the meeting was for lunchtime, didn't he?"

"Yeah. He was all revved up about it; reckoned he had something 'wicked' to show us."

Scobie's face performed a few of the usual contortions. It seemed to do that a lot when the conversation involved Razza.

Just then the man himself bounded into the room. "Scobes, maaate, sorry about that. Man, old Hackworth's really got it in for me. Kept me back after the bell. Went ballistic 'cause *he* reckons I wasn't paying attention in class when he was raving on about… well… whatever it was he was raving on about. Man, I'm being victimised."

"Well, you're here now, Orazio, so let's get started."

"No, wait up, Scobes. I got something to show you all. Dudes," Razz said, holding up his hands like a ringmaster, "prepare to be blown away." With that, he pulled out a sheet of paper from his pocket and began to unfold it.

"What's this?"

"*This*, Ishmael, is your passport to paradise. Man, I got sick of waiting for you, didn't I, so I did it myself. Yeah, that's right – I wrote a wicked love poem for you to send to Kelly Faulkner."

Bill, Prindabel and Scobie turned to me with an impressive display of synchronised eyebrow raising.

"Hey, don't look at me. This isn't my idea. I know

nothing about this, okay? Razz, maybe we can do this later – in *private*. We haven't got time now – Scobie wants to get the meeting started and Bill and Ignatius don't want to listen to some stupid love poem."

"I wouldn't mind," Bill said.

"It could be very educational," Ignatius added.

That just left Scobie.

"Never let it be said that I'm not a supporter of the arts."

"Cool!" Razza said. "Well, pin your ears back and get a load of this. It's called 'Hot or what!'."

"Can't you decide on a title?" Prindabel asked.

"Huh?"

"Can't you decide if you want to call it 'Hot' or 'What'?"

"It's not 'Hot' *or* 'What', Prindabel. It's 'Hot or what!'"

"Hot or what, *what*?"

"*What*?"

"What?"

"Maybe you should just start, Orazio," Scobie suggested.

"Yeah, right. Okay. Here we go. 'Hot or what!'" Razz said cautiously, with a glare at Prindabel.

"Like a microwave on high – you're hot!
Some chicks think they are – they're not!
They haven't got the bod you've got.
Man! Are you a total babe or what?

Your bod is hot but you are cool
You're deeper than a swimming pool
Man, you're the hottest chick in school
You fully rock and fully rule!

You're a smokin' babe – a 'sweet as' chick
You're hot to trot and fully sick
I'd give Kirsten Dunst the flick
Of all the chicks you'd be my pick!

You fry my brain, you turn me on
You light my fuse, 'cause YOU DA BOMB!"

When Razz finished, he slammed the poem proudly on the desk and folded his arms, ready to bask in the warmth of our praise. What he got was a chilly silence.

Scobie just stared at the paper on the desk with his mouth frozen mid-twist. Bill seemed to be in the process of undergoing an alien mind probe that as yet had failed to find anything of significance. I was trying to think of something to say, but somehow Razza's poem seemed to have sucked up my brain cells.

That left Prindabel. Throughout the reading he had sat glowering at Razza like a hawk. Now he looked from Bill to Scobie and from Scobie to me, pushed back his hair on his high forehead and frowned. Since it was obvious that no one else was going to speak, Ignatius Prindabel decided to give us his considered opinion.

"Well, that's just *crap*."

Razza's eyes widened and his jaw flopped open as if it had dislocated. "What?"

"That poem – it's just crap."

"Wh-what are you talking about, Prindabel?" Razza said, looking around for support. "It rocks – it's a wicked sonnet, man, just like the ones Shakespeare wrote – it's got fourteen lines and everything."

"Yes it has," Ignatius agreed. "Fourteen lines of *crap*."

"What would *you* know about poetry, anyway? It's got all the stuff Miss talked about – it's got your rhyme, your quatrains, your repetition, your imagery... man, it's even got similarities and a rhyming cufflink."

"Well, Orazio, I admit that I may not be an *expert* on poetry, but I know *crap* when I hear it. Oh, by the way, I think you might mean 'similes', not 'similarities'… and about your rhyming *couplet*, explain this to me: if *she's* the bomb like you say in the poem, then shouldn't *you* be lighting *her* fuse rather than the other way around, or was that just an example of your mixed metaphor?"

Razza threw up his hands in disgust. "Man, have you been tongue-kissing the USB ports on your computer again, Prindabel? Haven't you ever heard of 'poetic licence'?"

"What's that? A licence to kill poetry?"

Bill, Scobie and I exchanged a few secret glances. For once in his life Ignatius actually seemed to be holding his own against Razza.

"You know what I think your problem is, Prindabel? You've got too many calculators stuck up your arse to appreciate the *subtleties* of language. It's like Miss said – poetry is *condensed*, man – it's *compressed*. You gotta *study* it, look at it *closely*, to really dig it."

Ignatius appeared to consider this point seriously. "Perhaps you're right – a second reading may be in order."

Razza eyed Ignatius with suspicion then pushed the poem across to him. For the next couple of minutes Prindabel peered closely at the sheet before him, every so often raising his eyebrows, pushing out his lips and nodding thoughtfully. Finally he laid the poem carefully on the desk.

"Orazio, I think I might have been too rash in my judgment. I may have underestimated your special talent."

"All *right*, now we're getting somewhere..."

"Yes," Prindabel said solemnly, "this isn't just crap. This is crap of the highest order – crap distilled to its purest form."

"What?!"

Razza looked desperately around for backup. None came. He tried to speak, but Ignatius was like a man possessed.

"You know, when they finally discover the gene for crap – I predict it'll be this poem."

"What are you talking about, Prindabel?"

"I can't make it any plainer, can I? Your poem... is... gold-medal crap. I don't know how else to say it."

Scobie glanced across at Ignatius. "Blue-ribbon crap?" he put forward helpfully.

"Academy Award-winning crap," Bill chimed in.

"Top-shelf crap," Ignatius added.

And so began the inaugural St Daniel's College crap-a-thon as Bill, Scobie and Ignatius bounced ideas around the table.

"The Rolls Royce of crap."

"A-grade crap."

"The quintessence of crap."

"Premium-quality crap."

"Cutting-edge crap."

"The crap that other crap aspires to be."

"The pick of the crop crap."

"Crap's crap."

Then, when all the suggestions seemed to have dried up, Scobie raised his finger and showed a neat row of tiny white teeth.

"The *crème* de la crap!" he said triumphantly, and Bill and Ignatius nodded their approval.

Razza just stood there like road kill. Then he did the thing I'd been dreading. He turned to me. "Ishmael... What do you reckon?"

"Well... Razz... It's just... I just think... It's not that it's... you know... There's nothing really...

but you might need to… you know… Well…"

While I stumbled on, Prindabel scribbled something on a sheet of paper and held it up. It said: *Translation = It's CRAP!*

There was a stunned silence. The unthinkable was happening – Ignatius Prindabel was out-razzing the Razzman. It was like a prize fight, and the undisputed champion was now swaying on the ropes with bleary eyes.

"You talk about crap," Razza said. "Well, I'll tell you what's crap, Prindabel…"

It was the moment of truth. If the champ was going to avoid an upset, then now was the time to produce the killer punch. Razza's eyes flicked around to everyone at the table, then they carefully lined up Ignatius.

"*You're* crap – *that's* what's crap!"

Ignatius let Razza's barb sail harmlessly past his chin and then turned casually to Scobie. "Did you know that if you put a group of monkeys in a room with computers and keyboards and leave them there for eternity, it's a mathematical fact that *eventually*, just by *chance* and the laws of probability, they'll end up producing the entire works of Shakespeare?"

Razza groaned loudly. "And your point *is*, Prindabel?"

"No point, really," Ignatius said, turning to face Razza. "I was just wondering how many minutes it would take a baboon with a crayon to come up with your poem."

Razza went to speak but instead snatched his poem from the desk and stalked out of the room.

Ignatius locked his hands behind his head, put his feet up on the desk and rocked back on his chair smiling crookedly at us. "You know what?" he said happily. "I'm beginning to really like this poetry stuff."

13.
The Allure of
L'amour

I must admit, I did feel a little sorry for Razza. At the same time I was secretly pleased that Prindabel seemed to have successfully blown the whole crazy poetry idea out of the water. By lunchtime the following day I had pretty much convinced Razza that as 'wicked' as his plan was, it was time to let it go.

I blame Miss Tarango for putting it back on the agenda.

"Hi, boys. How did the debating meeting go?"

I glanced at Razza. "We kind of had to cancel it, Miss. We're trying again another time."

"Oh, too bad. You know, I'm counting on you boys

to lead the way again. You really put debating on the map at St Daniel's last year. We've got enough takers for four teams in the year below now, and the new juniors seem super keen."

There was a pause as Miss Tarango scanned the playground and asked a passing boy to 'pop' a bit of paper in the bin for her.

Then the Human Rip returned.

"Miss… you know what you said in class… about those dudes in Shakespeare's time sending love poems?"

I had a sickly feeling in my stomach. Someone was making balloon animals out of my lower intestine. "Razz… what're you doing?"

"Just asking Miss about poetry, all right? I mean, Miss… just say a guy today wrote a cool poem and sent it to someone he *really really* liked… do you reckon she'd think that was pretty wicked or what?"

Miss Tarango's eyes narrowed. "Orazio Zorzotto – you sly dog – don't tell me you've fallen victim to the allure of l'amour?"

Razza scrunched up his face.

"Have you been king-hit by Cupid, Orazio? Bitten by the love bug?"

"Me? Nah, no way, Miss – *him*."

He was pointing at me. A trapdoor had dropped open in the bottom of my stomach and all my balloon animal insides were sliding into my bowels.

Miss Tarango's eyes zoomed in on me. "Ishmael? Is this true? Have you abandoned me for another?"

My cheeks couldn't have burned more if I'd spent the night with my face wedged in a sandwich maker. I didn't think it could get much worse, but then Razza opened his mouth again and my personal life came pouring out of it like gravel from a tip truck.

"Yeah, 'fraid so, Miss. See, Ishmael's got the hots bad for this Kelly chick. He thinks she's perfect and everything. Only trouble is, she's sort of got this male model himbo boyfriend *Brad*, so what we thought was, if we could just write one of those love poems you've been talking about, she'd dump the Bradster and be all over Ishmael like sauce on a sausage roll. Is that a wicked plan or what?"

My life was flashing before my eyes like the highlights reel for *World's Worst Disasters Caught on Video*. I examined the ground between my feet and wondered how long it would take me to claw a hole deep enough to bury myself in.

"Orazio," Miss Tarango said, "would I be right in guessing that this 'wicked plan' is *your* 'wicked plan'?"

Beside me Razza was nodding enthusiastically.

"And what about you, Ishmael?" Miss Tarango said, turning to me. "What's your take on all of this?"

"I don't think it's such a great idea," I said.

What I really wanted to tell her was that, as an idea, I'd put it right up there with "Hey, let's strike a match and see if we can find that massive gas leak".

"He's just chicken, Miss. I even wrote a poem for him. It was awesome, but he won't use it – reckons Kelly wouldn't go for it or something. He's mad." Razza paused, then clicked his fingers. "Hey, Miss, maybe you could help us write something? Yeah, you'd know the kind of stuff that'd work, 'cause after all, you're a chi... I mean... you know... 'cause you're a gir... Well... you're a... You know... You're a..."

Miss Tarango's face set hard like porcelain and she held Razza firmly in her sights. "Careful now, Orazio," she said, "three strikes and I guarantee you'll be well and truly out."

Razza swallowed. "Well... you're like a... a female woman... and everything..." he said, forcing a smile.

"Ummmm… Well, I guess I can let you live… *this* time," Miss Tarango said as her dimples reappeared right on cue. "However, as for helping you write a declaration of affection for a young lady in poetry form, I think I might be out of my depth. But Ishmael, if you do decide to go ahead with this 'wicked plan', my only advice is, just be honest and sincere – be yourself – and don't do anything you're not comfortable with, even though *some* people we know, not mentioning any names, *Orazio Zorzotto*, might be very persuasive and persistent."

"Me, Miss? I'm just trying to help."

"Yes, well, no disrespect, Orazio, but maybe you could consider seeking out a more experienced and mature male perspective on these… affairs of the heart."

Razza considered this suggestion for a moment then said excitedly, "Hey, I know. We could ask Mr McCracken for help."

"Oh god, no!" Miss Tarango blurted out, then sort of froze. "Well… no… What I mean is… There's nothing wrong with Mr McCracken… He's a fine teacher, of course… It's just that you might need someone who's a little less… well, a little less…

Look, it's just that I think you might be better off with someone with a little more... a little more... Well... you know... someone that's... Someone who... Someone with... Well... Someone *else*."

It sounded like Miss Tarango had been taking lessons at the Ishmael Leseur School of Eloquence. I wasn't quite sure what she was getting at about Mr McCracken, but I knew why Razza thought he would be the man to see.

McCracken taught Maths and Economics and had quite a reputation at St Daniel's. For a start, he drove a customised ute that dripped with chrome *and* he played rugby for the State. His real claim to fame, however, in the eyes of the boys of St Daniel's, was the fact that every school function he attended he was accompanied by a different partner and each one could have been plucked right off the catwalk. As far as Razza was concerned, there was only one way to describe Clinton McCracken – 'Legend!'.

"Well, anyway boys, I have to get back to food-fight patrol – some of the natives are starting to get restless. So good luck, and Ishmael, don't worry too much about those male-model Fabio types, okay? They're usually not what they're cracked up to be... *believe* me. And this... Kelly, is it?... Well, if *you* really like her, then she must be something special, so if old what's-his-face hopes to hold on to her, he'd better have a lot more going for him than just looks. But you know what? My money's on you. I've got a feeling there's plenty of smart girls out there who'd find you pretty special too."

"Thanks, Miss." I knew she was probably just saying that to make me feel good, but the thing is... it made me feel good.

"Hey Miss, what about me? What do you reckon chicks think about me?"

"You, Orazio?" Miss Tarango said, holding her chin and curling her mouth to one side. "Well, you tell me. Do you honestly think there has ever been a female of the species born who could resist the magic and magnetism of the Zorzotto charm?"

Razza hesitated for a moment and then broke into a super-sized smile. "I doubt it, Miss. I *seriously* doubt it."

Miss Tarango shook her head slowly and laughed. There are some sounds that they should bottle and give to sick people. "You guys just crack me up," she said, and turned to leave.

Razza and I were both smiling and watching her walk away (perhaps a little more closely than we should have been) when she stopped and spun round. "Hey, I just had a thought. If you *did* decide to go ahead with the poem thing and you really needed some help, you know who you should see?"

Razza and I performed a dual head shake.

"Mr Guthrie."

We watched for a second as Miss Tarango wove her way across the playground. Then we turned to each other.

"Pele?" we said, screwing up our faces.

14.
Nyuk! Nyuk! Nyuk!

Unlike the Brazilian football star generally rated as the world's greatest ever footballer, Mr Guthrie was better known as an English/Geography teacher and our year's boarding master. He looked more like a trainee hippie, though. It was probably the dreadlocks that did it. The nickname 'Pele' stuck after his famous performance in last year's inter-house football tournament.

The lunchtime competition had been organised to celebrate the World Cup, with each of St Daniel's eight houses fielding a six-man team made up of one student from each year plus a teacher. Our team, the Charlton House Chiefs, made it to the final thanks mainly to our house master Mr Kryneborg, an ex A-grade player. The other thing we had going for us was the flair of our year's representative Orazio Zorzotto.

Our opponents were the Radley House Rockets. They were in the final because they had the strongest team and because their teacher representative was Mr Hardcastle, the St Daniel's sports master. It was difficult to miss Mr Hardcastle. He was stocky, with a chest like an over-sized granite boulder, a neck thicker than his number-three blade head and muscles that wrestled each other for space. When you added to that the tact of a wild boar, the sensitivity of a pile driver and the people skills of a rodeo bull, you had a man whose idea of getting in touch with his feminine side was pointing out when someone was "acting like a girl".

But it wasn't just Mr Hardcastle's intimidating physical presence that drove the Radley Rockets to the final. It was also his passionately held personal philosophy, which was summed up in the oft-repeated phrase, "losing is for losers". Another favourite mantra was, "I don't know the meaning of the word *fail*". The first time he said that in PE it prompted Razza to suggest to me (a little too loudly as it turned out) that

Mr Hardcastle probably didn't know the meaning of the word "brain" either. That was when Mr Hardcastle taught Razza the meaning of the word "push-up".

On the day of the big match, Mr Hardcastle and the Radley Rockets were at full strength, but Charlton House suffered a major setback – our star player Mr Kryneborg was away on a school excursion. A replacement teacher had to be found. That's where Mr Guthrie came in. At first it didn't seem too bad. After all, at least Mr Guthrie was young and looked pretty fit. But when he ran out on the field that day, I can't say our spirits exactly soared.

It wasn't just because Mr Guthrie's shorts looked like hand-me-downs from Andre the Giant or because his socks were bunched like ankle warmers on top of his no-name joggers or because his ropy dreadlocked hair was held back by an Amnesty International headband or even because he was wearing a T-shirt featuring a photo of the Three Stooges on the front with the words *Nyuk! Nyuk! Nyuk!* scrawled on the back. No, it was more the fact that during the pre-match drills, the ball seemed to bounce off or roll right past him every time he tried to control it. Razza, who was decked out from head to toe in his best AC Milan gear, spent most of the warm-up shaking his head.

By kick-off time, a big crowd encircled the field, with the Charlton and Radley supporters packing the grassy terraces on opposing sidelines. Miss Tarango joined us wearing a red Charlton House Chiefs T-shirt and carrying two balls of red crepe streamers.

"Show us your pom-poms!" Barry Bagsley shouted from up the back.

Unfortunately for Barry, the only things Miss showed him were her detention book and the way to Mr Barker's office.

Just before the match started, Miss Tarango addressed the Charlton boys sternly about being "good sports" and not getting too "carried away" with our support. She called for what she described as a "bit of decorum and class". I think it might have had something to do with the fact that the Principal, Brother Jerome, had just taken up a position beside her.

The scene was set. Scobie and the Charlton seniors launched into our war cry, and it wasn't long before both houses were trading chants and the teams were lining up for the kick-off. Mr Barker, the Deputy Principal, was the referee. There would be no disputed calls. He checked with both teams and blew the whistle.

The Chiefs were playing a kind of one, three, one formation with Razza as our lone attacking forward, followed by a three-man midfield, and Mr Guthrie as our last line of defence. I have to say this for Mr Guthrie, although he seemed to have all the style and athleticism of an intoxicated giraffe, you couldn't bag his effort. Whenever someone appeared about to break through or take a shot, he always managed to get some part of his body in the way – often painfully – and although he seemed to spend a lot of time sprawled on the ground, it worked.

The other thing you couldn't help noticing about Mr Guthrie was that he was enjoying himself. When he wasn't getting tangled up with Radley players and shaking his head and smiling in disbelief at how he had managed to stop another raid, he was encouraging and congratulating everyone around him – even the opposition. This, of course, was in stark contrast to Mr Hardcastle, who was charging around like Godzilla with a migraine barking orders so furiously that the big veins in his neck stuck out like garden hose.

As for Razza, within a few minutes of kick-off he'd succeeded in turning himself into Radley House's public enemy number one. This was partly because he was the obvious danger man, but mostly because of his tendency to fling himself dramatically on the pitch and call for a penalty every time an opposition player strayed within a metre radius of him. This finally came to an end when he backed into Mr Barker without realising it, performed a swan dive that even the Russian judge at the Olympics would have given a perfect ten and lay writhing on the ground clutching his ankle and moaning, "Do something, ref – I'm being hacked to pieces out here!"

Mr Barker did do something. He gave Razza a yellow card and five minutes in the sin bin.

When Razza asked why, Mr Barker said it was for "Conduct unbecoming of a halfway normal human being."

At the break the game was locked at one-all. Radley scored their goal when Razza was still off the field. Our goal had come just before half-time, and it was a Razzman special.

It started when one of our more skilful players,

Yousef Akmed, made a break down the right wing and hooked in a looping cross to Razza in space. At first it looked as if he was going to head it, but at the last second he leaned back slightly, braced himself and caught the full force of the ball on his chest. As his body absorbed the impact, the ball rebounded slightly, appeared to hover a moment in mid-air and then began to drop. In one blinding movement Razza stepped forward, planted his left foot on the turf, then drove through with his right boot, striking the ball firmly and squarely just centimetres from the ground. There was a sound like a sonic boom and the ball exploded off Razza's foot, rocketed dead straight for 20 metres, flashed over the top of the goalkeeper's outstretched hands before dipping wickedly like a tracking missile into the top corner of the net.

The Charlton supporters shot into the air and morphed into a bubbling mass of whooping, bouncing joy. Miss Tarango sprang up and let out a high pitched "Woooohooooooooooooo!" that had Brother Jerome wincing and covering his ears. Meanwhile Razza had pulled his shirt up over his head and was charging around the field with his arms spread out like a fighter plane – that was until he ran blindly into the mob of Radley supporters and was lucky to escape with his life.

The second half was a nerve-racking and intense battle with both teams having several chances to score. Razza tried every trick he knew, but following his spectacular first-half goal, Mr Hardcastle had set two defenders on him and now he was left with little room to move.

With about five minutes to go, it looked like a one-all draw was going to be the result, and I think most of us would have been happy with that. 'Most of us', of course, didn't include Mr Hardcastle. As well as 'fail', it's a pretty sure bet that you could add 'friendly' and 'fun' to the list of words Mr Hardcastle didn't know the meaning of. As the time ticked down he was becoming increasingly desperate and irritable with his team. Finally he just did it all himself. From a corner he used his massive height and weight advantage to out-leap and smother our defender and head home a goal for a two-one lead. I saw Mr Guthrie give a slight shake of his head as Mr Hardcastle brushed past him, pumping his fists and shouting at his team, "All right you lot – stay focused. We haven't won it yet!"

That's when the first of three weird things happened that had everyone in Charlton House turning to the people around them with their mouths dropped open. I'm surprised someone didn't start shoving ping-pong balls down our throats to win prizes.

What happened first was this. While the disorientated defender was being treated for what we all assumed was post-traumatic shock syndrome, Mr Guthrie jogged over to Razza and they began having a discussion about something. Even from a distance we could tell that Razza wasn't impressed. A few seconds later we knew why. When Mr Barker blew time, we did our famous sideshow alley impression.

What we saw was Orazio Zorzotto trudging unhappily off to fullback, leaving Mr Guthrie standing over the ball in the forward striker position waiting to kick off.

15.
Shoooooot!

Theories raged around the Charlton House supporters as we attempted to make sense of this bizarre and disturbing switch of positions. The general consensus was that Mr Guthrie had taken a knock to the head in one of his unorthodox tackles and was now clearly suffering from temporary brain damage.

Yet despite our confusion regarding the swap, we all agreed on one thing – we were doomed. Up front, our main strike weapon looked about as intimidating as a tranquillised kitten and seemed to be just hanging around waiting for the game to end. Even the Radley boys quickly realised Mr Guthrie was no danger and drifted off to cover the real threats.

According to Ignatius Prindabel, who had volunteered to be the official timekeeper, there was exactly one minute left to play when the second even weirder thing happened. Razza won the ball off Mr Hardcastle near our goal and looked up to see Yousef, with his hand raised, powering into open space down the right wing. Everyone knew it was our last chance to snatch a draw. Razza had already shifted his body weight back to chip the ball forward when a voice called clearly and firmly, "Orazio – now."

It was Mr Guthrie. He was standing alone just on the halfway line with his back towards the Radley goal. He was pointing to his feet. Two Radley defenders were zeroing in on Yousef. Razza hesitated, flashing his eyes from Mr Guthrie to Yousef and back. Then he grimaced before moving forward over the ball and drilling it along the ground. We all held our breath as a small synthetic sphere carrying all our hopes raced towards a man wearing baggy pants and a Three Stooges T-shirt.

Radley's left defender was the first to react. He sprinted towards Mr Guthrie's back as the ball closed in on its target. Mr Guthrie stuck out his right boot to trap it. The Radley fullback charged past him, obviously expecting to claim the rebound from Mr Guthrie's inevitable lack of control. But there was no rebound. And there was no control. The ball sailed right between Mr Guthrie's legs. By the time the Radley fullback realised what had happened he had well and truly overshot the mark, and Mr Guthrie was galloping in the opposite direction in hot pursuit of the ball with nothing between him and the Radley goalkeeper except 25 metres of grass.

Charlton House erupted in a communal roar of *Yeeeaaaaahhhhhh!* In front of me Miss Tarango suddenly dropped her pom-poms, latched on to Brother Jerome's arm with both hands and started to bounce up and down rapidly, shouting, "Go-go-go-go-go-go-*go!*"

Meanwhile, on the field, Mr Guthrie had caught up with the ball and was now stumbling and stuttering around as he nudged it jerkily in the general direction of the Radley goal.

Closing in fast behind him was Mr Hardcastle, screaming purple-faced at the keeper, "Come out! Come out! Close him down! Get out of there! *Come out!*"

The Radley goalie stood frozen for a moment, and then in sheer panic charged at Mr Guthrie. We braced ourselves for a collision. Miss Tarango buried her face in Brother Jerome's chest.

But then, just as they were about to clash on the edge of the penalty area, Mr Guthrie seemed to trip over his own feet, and as he staggered to regain his balance, his boot clipped the ball. Amazingly, as both he and the ball veered wildly to the right, the keeper slid harmlessly by on his left. Miss Tarango, roused by a huge Charlton cheer, looked up. Now there was only Mr Guthrie, the ball and an open goal. Miss Tarango embedded her long fingernails in Brother Jerome's arm and began to shake it furiously, screaming, "Shoot! Shoot! Shoot! *Shoooooot!*"

Mr Guthrie was inside the penalty area. Any half-reasonable strike and he would *have* to score, but he continued to totter and lurch and stumble all around the ball in an agonising tangle of boots. It looked as if he was trying to dribble the ball right into the net.

This was all the opening Mr Hardcastle needed. He burned up the last few metres, elbowed his way in beside Mr Guthrie and swung his right leg through to claim the ball – which he definitely would have done if one of Mr Guthrie's boots hadn't accidentally bumped against the ball again and sent it bobbling to the side. Now when Mr Hardcastle's boot sliced across the grass, all it collected were legs.

Later some people claimed that Mr Guthrie flew five metres through the air and somersaulted three times. Personally I think it was more like two metres and one somersault, but either way, the end result was that Mr Guthrie landed flat on his back in a cloud of dust... and he didn't move. Well, not until Mr Barker blew the whistle and pointed to the penalty spot. Then he sat up, rubbed his head, blinked a few times and climbed shakily to his feet.

As you can probably imagine, there was uproar from both sides. Miss Tarango, who had been staring silently with her hands over her mouth, suddenly burst into a raucous chant of, "Send him off! Send him off! *Send-him-orrrrrrrrrrrff!*" and she was about to march onto the field to deliver the message in person when Brother Jerome placed his big hand on her shoulder and gently eased her back.

Out on the pitch, Mr Hardcastle was waving his

arms about and informing Mr Barker that he "must `
be *joking*". Mr Barker just stood pointing at the penalty
spot. I'm sure I was wrong, but I thought for a moment
I saw him smile. While all that was happening,
Mr Guthrie was patting the Radley keeper on the back
and saying something about a "top effort" and being
"too good". Then he picked up the ball and tossed it to
Razza. "No pressure, Orazio."

Mr Hardcastle reeled around. "Hey, waaaiiiiit up
there, boyo. *He's* not taking it – no way. Only the player
supposedly fouled can take the penalty. It's in the
competition rules, and I should know, because I wrote
'em."

"Come on, John," Mr Guthrie said with smile, "it's
just a game. If you don't want Orazio, let one of the
other boys take it, then."

"Sorry, champ. It's you or no one. Them's the rules.
What sort of example would we be setting for the boys
if we just went about changing the rules when they
didn't suit us, eh?"

Mr Guthrie closed his eyes briefly then took the
ball from Razza. Mr Hardcastle turned immediately to
his keeper.

"Anthony, have a break from goal, matey. I'll take this one."

"But sir, I…"

"Yeah, I know, Tiger, but we just want to be sure, okay? Don't want to blow it now, do we? There's a good lad."

The Radley keeper moped slowly from the goal mouth and plonked himself down with the rest of his team on the halfway line. Miss Tarango glared across at Mr Hardcastle. I couldn't tell exactly what she was thinking, but I wouldn't have been surprised if the headline on the next day's paper had been, *St Daniel's Sports Master Instantaneously Combusts*.

We all waited for the final act to play out before us. While Mr Hardcastle bounced around on the goal line like an escapee from the primate enclosure of the zoo, Mr Guthrie moved to the penalty spot and stood behind the ball. Then he called Razza over. I was wondering what they were saying to each other when Mr Hardcastle's gruff voice cut across the field.

"Come on, *Pele*!" he shouted. "We haven't got all day. Or maybe you'd like Larry, Mo or Curly to take it for you?"

Mr Guthrie sent Razza back to join his teammates. Then he paced six large steps back from the ball, took two smaller steps to his left and stopped. After a deep breath and a slow exhale, he bent down and pulled up his socks. They were different colours. One had a smiley face on it. An outbreak of laughter came from the Radley camp. Mr Guthrie fixed his eyes on Mr Hardcastle, gave his dreadlocks a shake, then rocked forward and began his run in.

When Mr Guthrie reached the ball he drove his right boot through with a mighty force. Immediately everyone's eyes shot to the top left-hand corner of the net. This is where Mr Hardcastle's body was sailing. It was also where I'm sure the ball *would* have flown if Mr Guthrie had managed to middle it – which he most definitely hadn't. What he had managed to do was to catch the left edge of the ball with the outside of his boot, throw himself completely off balance and land on his backside.

And that's when the third and weirdest thing of all happened – the thing that would earn Mr Guthrie a place in St Daniel's folklore and brand him with the nickname *Pele*.

As the outside edge of Mr Guthrie's boot met the outside edge of the ball, instead of steaming through the air towards the *top left*-hand corner of the goal, the ball spun madly across the grass in an arc towards the *bottom right*-hand side.

As soon as Mr Hardcastle hit the pitch he realised that he'd dived the wrong way. Frantically flipping himself around, he scrambled on his hands and knees like some giant wind-up toy before hurling himself forward in one last despairing lunge.

Prindabel estimated later that he fell short by 13.5 centimetres. All Mr Hardcastle could do was watch in horror as the ball whirled past his scrabbling fingers and nestled safely in the side netting.

Radley House moaned.

Charlton House bellowed.

And Miss Tarango, to everyone's delight and with our Principal's blessing, performed a wild impromptu war dance on the sideline.

After the match, both team captains held aloft the inaugural St Daniel's World Cup Trophy and Brother Jerome, still nursing a bruised, battered and slightly punctured arm, made everyone line up for a group photo.

Mr Hardcastle and Mr Guthrie found themselves side by side.

"Of all the fluky shots," I heard Mr Hardcastle grumble.

"Nyuk, nyuk, nyuk," Mr Guthrie replied.

16.
Straitjackets-
R-Us

"**H**ey, dude, did you know that Pele has actually written some stuff?"

"What?"

It was a week since our conversation with Miss Tarango, and Razza and I were on our way to check out our year's noticeboard, which he insisted contained some important debating information.

"Guthrie – he's written some short stories and poetry and stuff. Been in magazines and everything."

"How do you know that?"

"Miss Tarango told me."

"Miss Tarango? Why have you been talking to

Miss Tarango about Mr Guthrie? Razz, I wasn't kidding when I said..."

"Yeah, yeah, I know. There's no way you'd ask Mr Guthrie to help you write a poem to Kelly. Man, I'm not deaf, you know – you've told me about a zillion times already. I just wondered why Miss even suggested him, that's all, so I asked her about it. No big deal. Thought I'd just mention it to you. You don't have a problem with that, do you?"

"No... I guess not." Just like I wouldn't have a problem with Dracula 'just mentioning' that I had a nice neck.

"Anyway... Maybe she was right. Maybe Guthrie might be a bit of a whiz with love poems and stuff."

"Razz, I couldn't care if he's Shakespeare's ghost writer. He doesn't even know me. I'm not asking him about writing a poem for Kelly Faulkner. No way. Besides, with my luck, his poetry writing would be right up there with his football skills."

Razza frowned and ran his fingers through his hair. "You see, that's another thing I've been thinking about. There was something suss going on there last year – how he kept us in the game and got the penalty for the draw."

"Yes, I think it's called 'dumb luck'."

"Yeah, I thought so too... once... but now I don't know so much. It's like... when you have *that* much luck, it doesn't seem that *dumb* any more... and then when you think about it for a while, it doesn't seem much like *luck* either."

"What are you talking about?"

"Well, I know that he looked pretty unusual out there, but the thing is, he *made* all those tackles, didn't he? And he *stopped* all those shots. And then, when we're behind and it looks like we're done for, he moves himself to striker. Now why would he do that if he was as hopeless as he was making out? And, dude, remember how he called for that ball and pointed to his feet?"

"Yeah, and missed it completely."

"Or dummied that defender dude cold and then dribbled around the keeper?"

"What? *Dribbled* around? You're telling me you think he meant to do that?"

"Maybe."

"Well then, if he's so brilliant, why didn't he just shoot straight away when he had an open goal? Even I could have scored from there."

"I was thinking... Maybe he didn't want to show up

the kid in goal… you know, make him feel bad. Maybe he was just waiting for Hardcastle to catch up the whole time, because he knew he could get the foul and win the penalty… only he thought someone else could be the hero and take it."

"So that penalty shot… you're not seriously suggesting that he did that… on *purpose*?"

Razza stopped walking and turned towards me.

"Remember how he called me over?"

"Yeah."

"You know what he asked me?"

"Nope."

"He asked me which way I thought Hardcastle would dive."

"So what did you tell him?"

"I told him left, top corner… and he said he thought so too. And *that's* the way Hardcastle went – left, top corner." Razza paused dramatically as if he was giving evidence in a murder trial. "But the *ball*, Ishmael, the ball ended up in the bottom right corner. Man, do you know how awesome you have to be to look that bad and still play great?"

"I don't get it. Why?"

"Why what?"

"Why do it? If he's so good, if he's such a great player, why didn't he just play normally? He could have scored heaps of goals and actually *won* the match for us instead of just drawing it."

"Yeah, I wondered about that too… and the only thing I can come up with is… maybe he didn't think it was all about him." Razza considered this for a moment, then shrugged and added, "Some people are weird like that."

I guess we were both wondering about Mr Guthrie and replaying parts of the game in our heads as we made our way through the senior block and up the stairs to the our year's level. When we arrived at the noticeboard I scanned it quickly.

"There's nothing here."

"Nothing where?" Razza said, looking around distractedly.

"Nothing on the board about debating."

"Debating? Oh right… you sure? Check again," Razza said, fiddling with his watch.

I worked my way around the timetables, messages, handouts, photos and lists of names. "Nope, nothing.

I told you Scobie would have let us know if there was some news."

"Sorry, man… I must have heard wrong."

"Well, *that* was a waste of time – let's go."

"Yeah… right… um… hey, wait up. Have you seen this?"

I moved closer to where Razza was peering intently at the noticeboard.

"What is it?"

"There's a notice here about the correct wearing of the school uniform. It says that shirts should be tucked in, trousers should be worn above the hips and that underwear should not be visible at any time. It says 'Underwear is underwear'. Now that's interesting."

This was bizarre behaviour, even for Razz.

"And did you know that sports uniforms can only be worn on *designated* sport days and that you have to bring your sports gear to change into for PE lessons but sports gear must not be worn to and from school? Man, I'm glad I got that cleared up. And look at this… Apparently the Maths department is offering morning and afternoon tutoring every Tuesday and Thursday leading up to the exams… But wow, check this out. Someone's calculator's gone missing... It says here he last had it in the..."

"Razz, are you all right?"

"Sure. Why?"

"Well, it's just that if you're about to say, 'Hey look, a timetable! Apparently all our subjects are on at different times and places each day during the week and this is how you work out where to go', then I think it might be time for a little shopping trip to *Straitjackets-R-Us*."

Razza was about to say something when a voice came from up the corridor. "Sorry, fellas. Hope you haven't been waiting too long."

Mr Guthrie was standing at the door to his form room. "Come on in."

I flashed a glare at Razza, who countered with a stupid toothy grin. "Well, you said that there was no way *you'd* ask Guthrie, so I thought you might like me to do it for you."

I breathed deeply and tried to keep myself together by picturing in my mind the excited huddle that would form around the noticeboard tomorrow morning.

"Hey, look at this," one of them would say. "Some boy had to be taken to hospital yesterday for emergency surgery. Apparently they found *The Complete Love Sonnets of Shakespeare* stuffed down his throat."

17.
Rigid!

Mr Guthrie looked at Razza and me from across the teacher's desk. On the wall behind him were big posters about recycling, alternative energy sources and global warming and on a long noticeboard beside him were dozens of newspaper articles with headlines on things like refugees, whaling, deforestation, homelessness, sweat shops and land rights. There were also two framed quotes. One was *No man is an island entire to himself* and the other one was *No snowflake in an avalanche ever feels responsible.*

"So, Orazio," Mr Guthrie said in his soft voice, "what's this 'serious problem' you said you both needed help with?"

I leaped in before Razza had a chance to open his sizeable mouth. "Sir, look, it's really not that important... We shouldn't even be here... Razz... Orazio shouldn't have bothered you... I told him not to... It's stupid... We're just wasting your lunchtime... We'll go... really, it's all right... We'll just go."

I stood up to leave and grabbed Razza by the shirt.

"Your choice, Ishmael. But I'm here now," Mr Guthrie said calmly, "and you've got me interested. Besides, lunch is for wimps, right? I'm embarrassed that I even brought this wimpy apple along. Anyway, they pay me such an enormous salary that I feel guilty taking time off to eat."

"Really, Sir? You teachers get paid lots, eh?"

Sometimes Razza wasn't quite on the same page as other people – often he wasn't even in the same library.

Mr Guthrie nodded. "Well, relative to ninety per cent of the world's population, Orazio, I guess you're absolutely right."

Then Mr Guthrie looked up at me. "So, Ishmael, what do you say? You want to stick around?"

I really didn't, but for some reason I sat down. Maybe it had something to do with the way Mr Guthrie smiled when he asked me the question or maybe it was because I knew he had the Miss Tarango seal of approval or maybe it was just that Razza didn't look like shifting and who knew what he would say or do if I wasn't there.

"Great. So tell me about this problem and how you think I can help?"

"Well, it's like this," Razza said, and then before I could stop him he was doing that tip-truck thing again, only the load seemed to have expanded this time around. "There's this chick called Kelly Faulkner that Ishmael's all freaked out over – you know, like he goes into la-la land every time he thinks about her – but apparently she's already hooked up with this Brad dude at the moment and he's like a macho sports jock, so naturally Ishmael thinks he's got no hope against him, you know, on account of the fact that the Bradster's like bigger, stronger, better-looking and a really cool guy as well. But then *I* came up with the awesome idea that Ishmael's *only* chance to win this Kelly chick over was to write her a wicked love poem – you know, like one of those sonnety things that Shakespeare and the other old poet dudes used to give to chicks in the prehistoric times to send them mental – only we need some help to get it just right."

Just in case you missed it, the topic of tonight's debate is, *That Ishmael Leseur is a complete loser*, and the first speaker for the Affirmative team was Orazio 'I don't know how to keep my mouth shut' Zorzotto. Now I would like to call on the Negative team to rebut. What, no rebuttal? Conceding defeat already?

Mr Guthrie shifted his eyes back and forth between the two of us. "*That's* your problem? You want help to write a poem... a *love* poem... to get a girl?"

"Yep," Razza said as if it rated right up there with widespread human rights abuses, the hole in the ozone layer, the rapid extinction of animal and plant species, the mass destruction of fragile ecosystems and the end of civilisation as we now know it.

Mr Guthrie shook his head so that his little sausages of hair wriggled about. "Well, I have to admit, boys, you've thrown me a bit. I was thinking along the lines of drug problems, maybe being tossed out of home and living on the street, in trouble with the police perhaps or targeted by the criminal underworld – that sort of thing. But poetry... this is *serious* stuff."

I was about to make another attempt to leave when Mr Guthrie turned to me.

"So, Ishmael, this girl, have you actually spoken to her? I mean, does she know you exist?"

I couldn't believe that I was talking to a teacher about Kelly Faulkner. "She knows I exist... but I'm not sure if she cares that much."

A smile came from across the desk. "Well, at least that's better than knowing you exist and wishing you didn't, right?"

"Naaah," Razza broke in, "Ishmael's got no idea, sir – I reckon she's secretly got the hots for him. Do you know that he rang her up once and when she answered the phone she *told* him, she actually *told* him, that she was practically nak..."

"Razz! Don't!... Ah... I mean... Aah... *Don't* you think... we should focus on the poem?"

Razza slumped back in his chair.

Mr Guthrie looked at both of us and tapped his pen on the desk. "Have you spoken to anyone else about this? Like your form room or English teacher?"

"That's Miss Tarango," Razza said, and Mr Guthrie's eyes flicked up. "Sure, we talked to her first, because that's where I got the idea from – 'cause we're doing sonnets and love stuff in English. But Miss didn't think she could help. She reckoned we needed to get a mature male perversion…"

"Per*spective!*"

"Yeah, right, what Ishmael said… Anyway, she said we should check it out with you."

The pen tapping stopped. "Zoe… Ah… Miss Tarango… suggested that you come and see *me*?"

"Yeah."

Mr Guthrie shuffled a few bits of paper around his desk and then picked up a big paper clip and began levering it apart until it looked like a lopsided silver heart. "Did she… she say why… Ah… Give a reason… at all?"

"Not really. She just said if we asked anyone for help it should be you – I guess because you're an English teacher and all, and then she told me you'd written some stuff yourself. She definitely didn't want us to go to Mr McCracken, I know that for sure. Man, she really gave him the flick."

"Mr McCracken?"

"Yeah, he was my first pick – sorry sir – but Miss wasn't hot on that idea at all. That's when she came up with you."

"So she... wasn't... that keen... on Mr McCracken?"

"No. Like I said, she reckoned we should speak to you."

"And not Mr McCracken?"

Razza shook his head.

"So she suggested me?"

"Yeah."

I had no idea what sort of a writer Mr Guthrie was, but I was beginning to have serious doubts about his comprehension skills.

"Right... good... right. Well, that's... good," Mr Guthrie said, glancing at the twisted paper clip in his hand and quickly dropping it in the bin.

The scrape of a chair on linoleum came from beside me. Razza had moved closer into the desk and was reaching into his shirt pocket.

"You're a writer, sir. Have a squiz at this," he said, pulling out a folded sheet of paper.

"Razza, what are you doing?!"

But it was too late. Mr Guthrie was already pressing the sheet flat on the desk. 'Hot or what!' was written at the top of the page in big red letters and decorated in leaping flames. I watched Sir's eyes widen as they made their way slowly down the lines. When he came to the end he sat in silence nodding his head.

"What d'ya reckon, sir? And it's all my own work. Don't you reckon if Ishmael sent that to Kelly it would do the trick? Don't you think it's totally wicked?"

Mr Guthrie looked as if he'd been asked to come up with a solution to global poverty by next Tuesday.

"Well, Orazio… it's um… You've um… There's um… certainly a lot of… *feeling* there… and I think… ah… you've developed a unique *voice*… and certainly your *theme* is… well, unmistakable…"

"You reckon Billy Shakespeare would be impressed?"

"Ahh, well… I think he would certainly be… *moved*," Mr Guthrie said, then added in a mumble, "I can almost imagine him rolling over as we speak."

"So what you're saying is, that it's fully sick, right, Sir?"

Mr Guthrie's eyes shot up. He looked like a drowning man who had just been tossed a lifeline. "Yes, Orazio, yes it is. That is exactly what I am saying. In my opinion your poem is literally… fully sick."

"Awesome!"

"In fact," Mr Guthrie said as he examined the words

in front of him as if he were attempting to break the Da Vinci code, "as far as degrees of *sickness* go, I think it could almost be described as… chronic."

"Chronic?" Razza echoed.

"Yes… and some might even go so far as to say that as a piece of literature… it is rigid with rigor mortis."

"Rigid! All *right*!" Razza shouted, turning to me and grinning like a maniac. "Did you *hear* that? Did you hear what Sir said? Sir reckons my poem is chronic *and* rigid. I *knew* it! Just wait till I tell Prindabel. He wouldn't recognise a poem if it jumped up and bit him on the dic—"

Razza looked over to Mr Guthrie and grinned.

"—*tionary*… Right… well… That's cool, then. See, I told you, Ishmael, but you wouldn't believe me, would you? Man, all we have to do now is whip my poem off to Kelly and everything'll be sweet."

Razza pushed his chair back and reached forward for the poem. "Thanks a lot, sir."

It was probably the look of horror on my face that caused Mr Guthrie to hold up his hand. "Wait, Orazio… there might be one *small* problem. As… *rigid*… as your poem is… it's still *your* poem, not Ishmael's. And I think if anyone's going to write this poem it should be Ishmael, don't you?"

Razza looked shattered. "Man, I spent nearly an *hour* writing that thing."

"That long?" Mr Guthrie said.

"Yeah, well, almost. I could only work on it during the ad breaks, 'cause you gotta really concentrate if you want to figure out whether they should go Deal or No Deal."

For a couple of seconds there, Mr Guthrie did a fine impression of Prindabel's 'abstract painting' response. Then he spoke as if he was coming out of a trance. "Okay... right... let's see... How about if you take this pen and paper, Orazio, grab yourself a seat at the back of the room and reel off an epic or two while I have a quiet word with Ishmael? How does that sound?"

Razza reluctantly agreed and I was left alone with Mr Guthrie.

"So, Ishmael – the old unrequited love? It's a bugger, eh? Well, you've come to the right place. That was my special subject at school. I was in the extension class for that, you know. Went on to do honours in it at uni. I'm still considered by many to be a leading authority." He smiled. I didn't mind Mr Guthrie at all. "So tell me… what's she like… this Kelly of yours?"

How could I explain to a teacher what Kelly Faulkner was like? How could I tell him that when she looked my way it was like everything inside me lit up and when she wasn't around I felt as grey and boring and pointless as a TV on standby.

"I dunno. She's like… She's like… perfect or something. I know that sounds really stupid."

'No… No, I don't think it's stupid at all. More like 'human'," Mr Guthrie said, and he looked as if he really meant it. "What did you notice first about her, then?"

"Well… she's got these eyes."

And Shakespeare reckoned *he* was a poet.

"All the better to see you with," Mr Guthrie said with a laugh. "Don't worry. I know exactly what it's like. It's really hard to find the words sometimes, isn't it?"

"I can *never* find them."

"Well, I'm no expert, but there's one thing I've learned – you can't force these things. Sometimes I think all you can do is wait, and then maybe when the time is right, the words will find *you*."

Could that be true? The only words that ever found me seemed to be the wrong ones.

"Look, Ishmael, I don't know if I can help you much. My only advice would be, if you did decide to write something, just keep it simple and straightforward. Don't worry about trying to be Shakespeare, and *definitely* don't try to be Zorzotto... just be yourself."

That's what Miss Tarango reckoned – that I should be myself. But it's not as easy as it sounds, and besides, what if just being me wasn't good enough?

Mr Guthrie and I talked a bit longer till the end of lunch – not just about poetry and Kelly Faulkner, but about some of the stuff on the posters and newspaper articles. When I left I didn't know whether I was any closer to solving my problems, but I was kind of glad that the planet had someone like Mr Guthrie worrying about it.

That night I actually did have a go at writing a poem about Kelly Faulkner, but it was useless – a bit like trying to catch a butterfly with a bear trap. Eventually I gave it away as a bad joke. Maybe Mr Guthrie was right: maybe what I needed to do was to wait and let the words find me.

I was still waiting a few weeks later when Barry Bagsley found me instead.

Track 4:
Pain

I got pain in my heart
Pain in my head
Pain in my body for you
I got pain I can't hide
Pain all inside
So much pain I don't know what to do

From The Dugongs: *Returned & Remastered*
Music & lyrics: W. Mangan and R. Leseur

18.
The Nerdman of
Alcatraz

In what surely must have been a personal best, Barry Bagsley had somehow managed to keep his major criminal tendencies under wraps for almost an entire term. I guess I should have realised that it was only a matter of time before something had to give. My only question was, why did it have to give all over me?

It started the day of our rescheduled debating meeting. Because things between Ignatius and Razza were a little tense following the infamous crap-a-thon episode, Scobie had decided that it might be a good idea to wait a while before trying again. So it wasn't until a couple of weeks out from the end of first term that we met in one of the library discussion rooms. Four of us sat around a table. This time we were waiting on Prindabel.

"He's probably off somewhere reading the Periodic Table for a laugh."

Bill and Scobie and I looked at Razza but no one replied. We just filed this last comment away with all the others he had suggested for Prindabel's absence. Like:

He'd been arrested for impersonating a human being.

He'd run off with a laptop dancer.

He was writing his autobiography – *The Nerdman of Alcatraz*.

I'm pretty sure Razza was just about to offer another possibility when Ignatius came stalking through the library and stepped awkwardly into the room. He was carrying some books and a plastic bag.

"Glad you could make it, Prindabel. What kept you? Were you delivering the keynote address at the International Geek Convention or something?"

"No. Our Pi Club T-shirts have just arrived. Had to collect mine from Mrs Mathieson."

"Pie Club? Geez, Prindabel, I knew you were weird,

but I didn't think you were into cooking. Are you planning on being the next Jamie Oliver? I can see it now… Ignatius Prindabel – The Nerdy Chef."

Ignatius started off giving Razza the old abstract painting look, but then a flicker of understanding appeared in his eyes. "No… Not *pie* as in p-i-e. *Pi* as in p-i."

Now it was Razza's turn to try the abstract painting look.

"Pi – the mathematical constant? Twenty-two over seven? Three-point-one-four to two decimal places? We did it in Maths. You must remember that."

Razza tilted his head and leaned forward slightly as if he was straining to recall.

"You know, the equation for the circumference of a circle – two pi r? The area of a circle – pi r squared?"

"Aaaaaaah riiiiiiiight," Razza said, not entirely convincingly. "So let me get this straight. You're in a club… based on a *number*?"

"That's right," Ignatius replied casually.

Razza's head began to shake and then he spread his hands wide as his face crumpled into total confusion. "But… *Why*?"

"It's not *just* a number," Ignatius said. "It's everywhere – in mathematics, physics, architecture, nature, art, you name it." Then he hovered over Razza like a bird of prey about to swoop. "Did you know that a team from the University of Tokyo has just calculated pi to 1.24 trillion decimal places? One-point-two-four trillion places! And guess what – I found out the other day that now you can order a poster from the internet that has pi calculated to the first *million* decimal places on it. My parents are getting me one for Christmas."

I don't think Razza could have looked more stunned if Ignatius had admitted to eating his grandmother.

"You're not even pretending to be normal any more, are you, Prindabel? You're nerd and proud."

Ignatius ignored Razza and pulled a white T-shirt from the plastic bag and held it up. "What do you think?"

On the front of the shirt was a big circle with the symbol for pi inside and lots of little 3.14s floating around it. It looked like this:

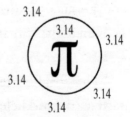

Ignatius flipped it over. On the back the words *I'm a Pi Man*! were printed in a large font above a drawing of a strange square-shaped pie with an 'A' baked on the crust and wisps of steam coming off it.

"You can buy one if you want. We're selling them to raise money to buy badges and coffee mugs for International Pi Day next year."

"International Pi Day?" Razza said. "Now I know you're making all this up."

"It's true. The 14th of March – 3rd month, 14th day – see, like 3.14, although it can be celebrated on the 22nd of July because that's 22/7. It just depends on whether you write the date with the month first or the day first. There are pi clubs all around the world."

Razza swallowed hard. "You mean... there are others... out there... like *you*?" He pointed a shaky finger at Ignatius. "Why have you come here? What do you want? This is *our* planet. Leave us alone. We-will-not-go-quietly-into-the-night!"

"I take it that that means you won't be purchasing a T-shirt."

"Prindabel, I'm telling you, man, there are nuclear-powered vacuum cleaners that don't suck as much as that shirt. Perhaps you could try me again later... maybe sometime around Halloween or when I'm feeling more in the mood for committing fashion suicide, okay?"

A loud and deliberate clearing of a throat cut across the room. Bill, Ignatius, Razza and I looked at Scobie, who was sitting at the far end of the table.

"Debating meeting? Remember?"

"Sure, Scobes. No worries," Razza said. "I've just got one last question for our interplanetary visitor." Then he jabbed his finger at the bizarre drawing on the back of the shirt. "Prindabel, what exactly is *that*?"

"An apple pie," he said, making a face to show that he thought the answer was obvious.

"Aren't pies supposed to be *round*?"

Ignatius leered at us all with a grin like a deranged barracuda. "No," he said. "Pie – are – squared!"

Razza immediately slumped back as if he'd been shot, tumbled from his chair and lay on the floor groaning. The only other noise in the room was the sound of air being sucked rapidly in and out between two rows of pointy teeth.

You could have been excused from mistaking it for a hyperventilating steam train, but it wasn't. It was just the Prindabel version of laughter.

19.
A Big Pink Comet

"**H**ey, Ishmael. You're an evil dude, man – you've made the overdue book list. From tomorrow you start paying fines and your borrowing privileges will be suspended. Hope my mum doesn't find out that I've been mixing with such a bad influence."

The debating meeting had just broken up and we were heading out of the library. I turned back and saw Razza reading from a sheet that was pinned near the checkout desk.

"Really? What book?"

"Ah… *Kissing for Dummies*," he shouted out as heads bobbed up from reading carrels and the Librarian

Mr Fitler glared from the shelves. "No... wait a minute... I read the wrong line. It's actually *Great Rainforests of the World*."

"Oh... right... The Geography assignment. I forgot about that. It's up in our form room."

I checked my watch. I had five minutes before the end of lunch.

"Razz, I'm gonna shoot upstairs and get it now. I'll catch you in Science."

As it turned out, I didn't make it back to the library and I didn't catch up with Razza in Science either. My day was about to take a dramatic turn. I was about to put Barry Bagsley out of action for two weeks with just one punch.

It happened like this.

As I swung into my form room, three heads bobbed up simultaneously to greet me. Fortunately they were each attached to a different body. Unfortunately, those three bodies belonged to Doug Savage, Danny Wallace and Barry Bagsley. They stood huddled around an open desk.

Barry greeted me like a long-lost friend. "Le Sewer, we're busy here, so rack off," he said, jutting his jaw towards the door as he spat out those last two words.

Danny Wallace lowered the desk lid with a sly grin.

"I just gotta grab something." Without waiting for a reply I wrenched open the lid of my desk and dug out the missing book. It was then that I realised exactly what they were crowded around.

"What're you doing?"

"None of your business, Manure. Now like I said, rack off."

"That's Bill Kingsley's desk."

"Well, so it is."

"What are you doing to it?"

"Giving it a spring clean – adding some decoration."

Barry Bagsley smiled and turned to Wallace and Savage, who laughed. "Go ahead. Let's see what Le Spewer thinks of our masterpiece, boys. It would be good to have an unbiased opinion."

Danny Wallace lifted the lid and all three of them grinned madly. Stuck on the underside was a blown-up picture of Bill Kingsley. It came from one of last year's school newsletters when our debating team made the semi-finals. Someone had obviously been at it with Photoshop. Bill Kingsley's body had doubled in size and now he was holding a bloodied head in his hands. Above the image a large caption read, Dill Kingsize Wins Debate by Eating Opposition.

"What d'ya reckon? Not bad eh, Le Spewer?"

All I could think of was the look of misery plastered on Bill's face last year when Barry and the others had tormented him about his weight.

"Take it down."

Barry Bagsley looked as if he didn't understand. "Now why would we want to do that?"

"He's never done anything to you. Take it down."

"Sorry, Piss-whale – not gonna happen. Unless you think you can make us."

I moved closer to the desk. Danny and Doug were on the other side. Barry Bagsley was right in front of me. I had no idea what I was going to do.

"Look, just take it down. It's not funny."

"What d'ya mean, not funny? Where's your sense of humour, Manure? It's hilarious."

"Not for Bill."

"Well it's staying, so I guess the thing is… what are you gonna do about it?"

Good question. I remembered what I'd promised

myself last year. No more hiding. No more being invisible.

"If you don't take it down I'm going to Mr Barker."

Barry Bagsley curled his lip into a sneer. "That'd be right, run to Barker. You know what I think? I think you're a gutless wimp."

"I don't care what you think. Take it down or I go to Mr Barker."

Barry Bagsley looked me over. He didn't seem that impressed with what he saw. "You're sounding pretty brave all of a sudden, Piss-whale. Wouldn't be because you think mutant-boy Scobie will save you, would it?"

"Yeah," Danny Wallace weighed in, "are you gonna run to your big *bwuvver* for protection?"

Doug Savage grunted, "*Little* brother."

Two connecting words. This was a breakthrough for Doug. We really should have done something special to mark the occasion. A cake, perhaps.

A hiss of air escaped through Barry Bagsley's teeth. "Scobie? Who'd wanna be related to that freak?"

I looked at the sneering, arrogant face before me. My fingers began to close into a hard, angry ball.

"I wouldn't mind being related to Scobie," I said as

my fingernails dug into my palms, "but if I was *your* brother, I'd want to kill myself."

I watched Barry Bagsley's eyes closely as they quivered then set hard.

Of course, in hindsight, what I *should* have been watching was his right fist, which at that very moment was hurtling towards my face like a big pink comet.

20.
Game Over, Man!

The first indication that Barry Bagsley's fist had crash-landed on my head was a hot spear of pain that shot up my nose and embedded itself somewhere deep behind my eyes.

I don't think I saw stars. It was more like a massive solar flare, then everything went blurry. Suddenly my nose felt about as big as Tasmania and my left eye began to throb and water. Then a warm dampness oozed over my lips and chin. I cupped my hand lightly over my mouth, and it came away dripping with blood. I looked down. Big blotches of bright red were splattering the floor like an aerial bombing raid.

That's when I blanked out.

Apparently Mr Guthrie, who just happened to be passing by, was the first on the scene. Barry, Danny and Doug were sent immediately to Mr Barker's office and when I came round Mr Guthrie took me straight to sick bay and later to the boarders' infirmary where the nurse checked me over. My nose wasn't broken, just badly bruised. Over the next few days the area around my left eye changed from a lovely shade of purply-black to sickly yellow.

Of course Mr Barker conducted a very thorough investigation into the whole affair, which resulted in Barry, Danny and Doug owning up to making the picture of Bill. Barry also admitted to punching me, but wouldn't say why, except that he "felt like it". As you can imagine, Mum and Dad were pretty upset, but after a meeting with Mr Barker and the Bagsleys they seemed calmer about the whole thing. I'm not sure what was said there. Mum just told me everyone agreed that what Barry did was wrong. (Der – really?) Then she added that the Bagsleys were "nice people" and that there are "two sides to every story". Two sides to every story? The only two sides I could see were my nose and Bagsley's fist.

Anyway, the wash-up of it all was that Danny and Doug each copped three afternoon detentions and Barry got a two-week in-school suspension. This meant that he spent all his lessons either outside Mr Barker's office or with the school counsellor Mr Devlin. Also, in order to avoid all contact with other students, he was scheduled on for different lunchtimes.

"Suspension's not too bad," Marco Armbruster informed us in registration on the first day of Barry Bagsley's absence. "I got a week the time I flattened that Parkville jerk at rugby. Jerome reckoned I brought the school into destitute or something, which was crap. That clown deserved it. You should have heard the sicko stuff he said about my sister when we packed a scrum… 'Course it was all true, but that's beside the point, eh?"

Razza and I looked up at the solid ball of muscle that was Marco Armbruster. It wasn't quite 9 a.m. and already a five o'clock shadow was darkening on his chin.

"Just boring, mainly – doing school stuff all day. Worse part is Devlin. Wants to talk all the time. Then he makes you write down ya feelings. Once he said I should write a poem. A poem! Supposed to help me get in touch with my emotions so that I could understand why I did what I did. Well, that Parkville loser was asking for a bashing – so I bashed him. How do you make a frigging poem out of that?"

Razza and I shook our heads in sympathy. Yes, even Shakespeare might have struggled with that one.

"Hey Marco," Razza said as he twirled his biro with dizzying speed through his fingers, "… just as a point of interest… how old's your sister, then?"

Marco Armbruster trained his ink-spot eyes on Razza.

"Zorzotto, my sister would eat you alive for breakfast and still have room for her Weetabix," he said, before turning and ploughing through the crowded classroom like a slow-moving wrecking ball.

"Marco! Wait!" Razza shouted after him. "I'm cool with that – bring a photo! Or a video would be good! Is she on Web Cam by any chance?"

Marco made no attempt to respond except by making a sign with his hand over his shoulder as he walked away, so Razza swivelled back around and started drumming an intricate rhythm on the desk. "Man," he said as he maintained the beat, "that eye of yours is something else. I can't believe he hit you – at *school*.

You sure you didn't take a swing at him first?"

"Do I look like a crazy person to you? I told you, all I said was, if he was my brother I'd kill myself – then wham!"

"That's all? Doesn't make sense, man." Suddenly Razza stopped drumming. "Hey, you know what you oughta do? You oughta let Kelly see that eye."

"What? Why?"

"Dude, chicks dig that sort of stuff. Makes you look all macho – bet Brad baby is covered in cuts and bruises all the time from footy. You reckon Kelly doesn't get off on that?"

"Razz, have you ever thought of consulting one of our highly trained mental health experts?"

"Hey, just remember what happened when she found out about you sticking up for her little brother? Well, I'm telling you, dude, if Kelly got a load of that eye of yours and heard about how you were creamed by *three* guys just because you were trying to help out a mate – man, you know what'd happen? She'd go weak at the knees and then she'd get that dopey, dreamy look chicks get on their faces like they're about to throw up, and then… that'd be it."

"That'd be *what*, exactly?"

"That'd be Game Over, man!" he said and went back to his mad drumming.

It took a few days for the swelling and pain to go out of my eye – the bruise hung around for quite a bit longer. It was almost worth it, though. That punch earned me (and everyone else) two glorious, fun-filled weeks in a Barry Bagsley-free zone.

What I didn't know was this. I was about to have two more close encounters with Barry, and both of them would send me reeling and leave a deeper, more lasting impression than any black eye.

21.
Moved to Vomit

The first of the two encounters occurred at lunch on the last day of the term. I was called to a classroom where Mr Barker was supervising Barry Bagsley for the final time before he was to be tagged and released back into the wild.

When I walked into the room Barry was sitting at the back, writing. Mr Barker was behind the teacher's desk. He looked up and called me over. "Mr Leseur, come in. Mr Bagsley, would you care to join us?"

Barry moved slowly to the front. He looked about as happy as a Hell's Angel at a craft show. We both stood there as Mr Barker explained a few things we needed to be "absolutely clear about". Things like: that there was no place for physical violence or bullying at St Daniel's; that any problems or disagreements we had should be settled like reasonable, intelligent human beings, not cavemen; that he and Mr Devlin and all the other teachers were there to help; that this whole "unsavoury" incident was now over; and that there would be no repeat performances otherwise the consequences would be "swift and severe".

I nodded my head in agreement with everything Mr Barker said. Barry Bagsley stood motionless with a face like a death mask. I tried to convince myself that he was nodding on the inside.

When he'd finished his spiel, Mr Barker told Barry he was free to go and he returned to his desk, grabbed his pens, shoved some sheets of paper roughly into a Manila folder, slung his bag over his back, and left without a word. Mr Barker kept me there a while longer. I guess he wanted to put a bit of distance between Barry and me. I wasn't about to complain.

"I sincerely hope, Mr Leseur, that you are not considering pursuing your pugilistic ambitions."

"Sir?"

"Boxing, Mr Leseur – you're not thinking of taking it up as a career, are you?"

"No, Sir."

"A wise decision. Nonetheless, if there is even the slightest possibility of a rematch or trouble of any kind, I expect to be informed immediately."

"Yes, Sir."

Mr Barker jotted a few words into his diary and slapped it shut. When he looked up at me I can't say he smiled exactly – it was more like a less intense scowl. "You and Mr Kingsley are friends?"

"Yes, Sir."

He waited a moment, then clicked the top of his pen and slotted it into his shirt pocket. "Then he is indeed a fortunate man. You may go, Mr Leseur."

I closed the door behind me and headed towards the steps. I wanted to get outside. I wanted to find Razza and Scobie and forget all about Barry Bagsley. But halfway along the corridor, a sheet of paper on the floor caught my attention. I recognised it as paper from the counsellor's office. Mr Devlin's name and contact details were at the top. I picked it up for a closer look. Most of the page was filled with scribbles and doodles except for a patch at the bottom where someone had been practising their signature.

I flipped the sheet over. On the back were six or so lines of writing. A hard pen stroke had been slashed across them but the words were still clear. I had only begun to read them when a hand flashed over my shoulder and snatched the page away.

"What have we got here, Leseur? Haven't been passing notes in class, have you? Or maybe it's a love letter to little Scobie-Wobie, eh?"

It was Danny Wallace, and beside him gazing dumbly like a reject from the Stone Age was Doug Savage.

"Oh, lookie here, Dougy. Leseur's written a poem, and it's called 'Why?'. Awwwwwwww." Danny placed his hand over his heart, fluttered his eyes and began to read.

Why – couldn't it have been me, not you?

Why – couldn't you stay strong?

Why – won't you ever come back?

Why – can't we ever do stuff together?

Why – will I never see you again?

Why – couldn't I help you like you always
helped me?

When he'd finished, Danny shoved his index finger in his mouth and pretended to throw up. Danny Wallace was a master of mime.

"Leseur, I am seriously moved to vomit. What is this crap? Writing about one of your *bum* buddies, are you? I guess you…" Then something caught his eye behind me. He lifted his chin a little and called down the corridor, "Hey Bazz, over here. We've been looking for you."

Barry Bagsley had just come up the steps at the far end of the corridor and now he was heading our way. He still had his bag over his shoulder and a folder with pages sprouting from it clutched in one hand.

"Check this out – Le Spewer's been writing love poems to a *special* friend."

Danny read the poem again with extra passion and expression while Doug Savage snuffled and snorted beside him like a bulldog with sinus problems. I watched Barry Bagsley's face darken and harden. Only his eyes revealed any real emotion.

"Geez, now I know why you're called Le *Spewer*," Danny Wallace said when he'd finished his second recitation. "You got any more of this puke?"

He started to turn the page over to look on the other side, but before I really knew what I was doing I had grabbed it away from him. "Give it here."

"Woooooooooo – bit touchy are we, Leseur? So it is yours, eh?"

"What if it is?"

"Well, we're huge fans of your stuff and we'd just *love* to read some more, wouldn't we, guys? Come on, hand it over. We want to hear more of Manure's manure."

"No."

"Hey, Barry, Le Spewer isn't sharing. What do you reckon we should do?"

Barry Bagsley eyeballed me for a long time before replying in little more than a whisper. "Nothing... He'll keep."

"What? But..."

Barry shifted his cold eyes on to Danny Wallace. "I *said*... he'll *keep*. You got a problem with that, Wallace? What about you, Savage?"

Danny and Doug remained silent. Then Barry jerked his head towards the steps and they were both forced to tag along behind as he led them away.

I waited until they had all disappeared from sight. When I knew I was finally alone, I looked around me. Everything seemed the same – same corridor with classrooms on one side and windows on the other, same scuffed tiles on the floor, same class photos along the wall, same playground out the window, same sounds, same smells. But I knew there was something much deeper that just wasn't the same any more.

I walked to the end of the corridor and sat on the steps that led down to the ground floor. In my mind I replayed everything that had just happened trying to make some sense of it all, but no matter how many times I worked my way through it, there were always three things that just didn't seem to gel together.

First, there was the poem that Danny Wallace had read out. Second, there was the strange swirling mix of anger and fear I had seen in Barry Bagsley's eyes as he listened to it. And the third thing? The third thing was the twenty or so signatures scrawled on the back of the sheet of paper that I still held in my hand.

The ones that said *B. Bagsley*.

22.
A Good Thing
to Know

My second encounter with Barry Bagsley occurred
that same day after the end-of-term assembly,
and it would make all our previous meetings seem like
discussions about the weather.

I was on my way home, halfway down the cement
path that ran between a creek and the row of five
football fields imaginatively referred to by everyone at
St Daniel's as 'The Fields', when a cold voice called
from behind me.

"Leseur."

I froze, then turned around. Barry Bagsley was
leaning against one of the large pine trees that lined the

path. I did a quick survey of the surrounding area. Usually there were loads of boarders mucking about with a football or something, but not today – they had all escaped home for the break. It suddenly struck me how quiet and empty it was. What was it Razza had said about Barry being more likely to biff someone when it was deserted? My nose started to tingle as if it was trying to find a place to hide.

"Look, I don't know what you want, but…"

Barry Bagsley cut me off. "Why did you do it?"

"What…"

"I want to know why you did it."

"What do you mean? Did what?"

"You know. Why'd you let Wallace and Savage think you'd written that poem… when you knew it was me?"

"I… I don't know."

I didn't either. I could have easily told them it wasn't my poem. I could have shown them the signatures on the sheet. Even Danny and Doug would have had just enough brains between them to work out who it belonged to. So why didn't I? Why did I protect someone who had made my life and Bill Kingsley's life a misery? Someone who had used my face as a punching bag?

Barry Bagsley continued to stare at me in silence.

I didn't know what to say or what to do. Then I remembered that I still had the poem in my top pocket. I took it out and held it towards him. "Here."

He pushed himself off the tree and moved slowly towards me. There was less than half a metre between us. He took the folded sheet of paper, held it briefly in his hand and closed his fist tightly around it. My eyes began to sting as I recalled the searing pain that fist was capable of. He spoke without looking up from the wad of paper in his hand.

"It's stuff Devlin made me write."

I think that was the first thing Barry Bagsley had ever said to me that didn't contain an insult. But there was more to come... much more.

"It's about my brother," he mumbled. "... Older brother... He died... 'bout four years ago... Leukaemia."

My head was spinning. This wasn't right. This wasn't the way things went. Barry Bagsley was talking to me and he wasn't sneering or swearing or putting me down or mashing my name into pulp. He was telling me about his brother... his *dead* brother. I thought about Prue. What if something happened to her? What if...

I looked at the mop of blonde hair and the broad shoulders in front of me. I wanted to say something, but my thoughts wouldn't form into words.

"That's... I... I'm..."

"That's why I hit you."

At first I didn't understand what he meant – I couldn't see any connection. Then I remembered what I'd said that day – about how I'd kill myself if I was his brother – and it felt like someone had put their fist through my stomach.

"Look, I... I didn't mean... I'm sorry... about what I said... and about your brother."

Barry remained still and the muscles in his jaw tightened. I could hear him breathing. Then he lifted his head and clamped me with an icy glare. "If you tell anybody... anyone at all..."

"I... I won't... I wouldn't do that... I wouldn't tell anyone... ever."

He scanned my face like an X-ray machine.

"I didn't tell about the poem," I said finally.

We stood facing each other like inhabitants of different solar systems. Then Barry Bagsley moved away, collected his bag from beside the tree and hoisted it over his shoulder. He was leaving, but I had my own question to ask.

"Barry."

He looked back at me.

"Lay off Bill Kingsley?"

"Or what?" he said as he pushed the poem into his pocket.

"Or nothing. I'm *asking* you... please."

He looked hard at me. "Why is it such a big deal to you what happens to Kingsley, anyway?"

"Because he's my friend... and he doesn't deserve it... Nobody does."

Barry Bagsley's eyes drilled into mine. "We're even, then," was all he said before turning and setting off across the field.

He kept his word. From that day on, Bill Kingsley stopped being bullied and started to remember how to smile. And something between Barry and me changed as well. Don't get me wrong – it's not like we became best mates or anything, but at last I found that I could breathe in his presence and I didn't have to be invisible any more. I could just be me.

As I continued my journey home that day it felt like

the weight of my school bag was the only thing keeping me from floating away. After all the facts and theories and ideas my teachers had tried to cram into my head, the most important thing I'd learned from my first term of this year was this: Life can change. Sometimes it gets better. It was a good thing to know.

During the mid-year break life changed again. My father kind of disappeared.

Track 5: Memory Sea

One day I turned around and you were gone
They said that's how it is, life must go on
But every now and then I float away
And find myself adrift in yesterday

Chorus
And I'm drowning in a memory sea
I'm drowning in a memory sea
I'm drowning in a memory sea
But no one there can rescue me.

From The Dugongs: *Returned & Remastered*
Words & lyrics: R. Leseur

23.
Philopatridomania

Dad did his vanishing trick during the second week of the holidays after Mum called out, "Ron, you've got an email from Ray."

Ray was Uncle Ray, who wasn't really our uncle, but a friend of my parents from their university days. He used to be around a lot when Prue and I were little, but we hadn't seen him for years.

I was having breakfast in the kitchen at the time when Dad wandered down the corridor in his pyjamas with his curly red hair sticking up at bizarre angles like a dried mop. I watched him enter the study.

And that's when he disappeared.

Not that he was beamed up by aliens or anything really exciting like that. I mean, he did walk back in a bit later and he *looked* the same. But it just wasn't the Ron Leseur I knew – not the one who loved to tell stories and pathetic jokes, the one who had dressed up as Captain Ahab when Mum was pregnant with me just because she said she looked like a whale; the one who made her laugh so hard she gave birth and the one who called me Ishmael after the narrator of *Moby Dick*.

The man who came out of the study that morning didn't say a word – just looked right through me as if I didn't exist – like there was just a bowl of cereal at the table eating itself. At dinner that night he was still in zombie mode and afterwards he just sat by himself clutching his acoustic guitar and playing his old Beatles records. That's where I found him the next morning. He was still wearing headphones, and he looked up at me with bleary eyes and said in a croaky voice, "It was 20 years ago today," then drifted off to sleep.

When I asked Mum what was wrong with him, she didn't seem very talkative, so I decided it was time to seek expert help.

"He listened to Beatles records all night and then he said *that*?"

My little sister Prue was sitting cross-legged on the end of my bed. She looked at me over the top of her narrow rectangular reading glasses. "This could be serious."

"Serious? What do you mean?"

She dropped her copy of *A Brief History of Time* on the bed and placed her glasses on the cover. "Well, it sounds like philopatridomania."

"What?"

"Philopatridomania – it means extreme nostalgia."

"Nostalgia? That's not too serious, is it?"

"It could be. I read a book on the history of medicine once, and do you know that in the seventeenth century nostalgia was treated as a legitimate medical condition? A Swiss doctor – I think his name was Hofer – identified it. He was the one who came up with the name *philopatridomania*. Anyway, that's beside the point, but back then nostalgia *was* taken seriously. Hofer identified it as the pain someone feels when they fear they'll never see their native land again. A lot of soldiers fighting in foreign countries were diagnosed with it – they claimed quite a few *died* of it."

Prue peered back at me. I tried to imagine how much information was jammed into that cute near-genius head.

"But that doesn't make sense – Dad's *in* his native land."

"Yes, but it's not just about land any more – it's about anything that you think you'll never see again. And there are some doctors today who believe that maybe Hofer was on the right track, and maybe we should treat extreme forms of nostalgia as a serious medical condition as he did."

"What... so Dad's suffering from a rare strain of Beatle nostalgia... because he'll never see them again?"

"Umm... Beatle-philopatrido-mania perhaps," Prue said with quick grin. "Look, it all fits, doesn't it? First he goes all comatose, then he plays Fab Four all night and then this morning he comes out with, "It was twenty years ago today". There's a definite pattern going on here."

"But I don't get that last bit. The Beatles were mainly around in the 1960s, right? So that'd be closer to forty years ago, not twenty."

Prue gaped at me. "It's comes from a Beatles song,

you durr. It's *only* the opening line of the title track of *Sergeant Pepper's Lonely Hearts Club Band*, possibly the most famous album of all time."

"Oh… right… I'll take your word for it. But why's he suffering from nostalgia now? Dad's *always* had a thing about the Beatles and he was fine… until he got that email from Uncle Ray."

Prue picked up her glasses and sucked on the… well… whatever you call that end bit that you loop behind your ear… the handle, hooky bit thingy.

"It could be that Uncle Ray mentioned something about the Beatles in his email… or maybe what he wrote reminded Dad of something from the past, who knows? Anything could have triggered it off."

It was hard not to agree with Prue. After all, even though she was over a year younger than me, she *was* an official near-genius *and* one of the world's leading authorities on the Beatles.

I guess you might find that last bit hard to believe, but it's true. In fact, according to Dad, it was the Beatles who were responsible for turning Prue into a near-genius in the first place. They also named her.

And they saved her life.

24.
How-Prue-got-the-name-Prue

It all happened when Prue was born. Unlike me, she arrived early rather than late. Very early. More than three months early. As she lay in her incubator Dad says she looked like a little red doll trapped in a tangle of tubes. My parents were told to prepare for the worst – and I guess that's what Dad did.

While Mum recovered in a hospital bed, he set up a permanent camp beside Prue in the premature babies' room reciting his favourite poems to her, reading from his favourite books and playing his favourite music – with Dylan and the Beatles on high rotation. Mum says Dad hardly slept for three days and then only when the nurses and doctors forced him to by promising they would keep the music playing.

It was on the fourth day that things "took a turn for the worse" and it was "touch and go" whether Prue would make it through the night. The doctors said that they had done everything they could and now it was up to her.

That night Dad played his entire Beatles collection and read aloud for hour after hour, until sometime early in the morning he must have dozed off. When he woke up he says everything was still and quiet except for the music. Then Dad leaned forward and peered in through the clear plastic side of the incubator. Prue's tiny heart was still beating – and if you believe my father, it was beating in time to the tune that was floating around the room. The Beatles were singing, "Dear Prudence", and as Dad watched and listened, his baby daughter slowly opened up her eyes and greeted the brand new day.

I'm sure Dad loves the "how-Prue-got-the-name-Prue" story just as much as the "how-Ishmael-got-the-name-Ishmael" story; he just doesn't talk about it as much. I like it too. I don't know if it all happened exactly like my father describes it – Dad has a tendency to 'improve' things when he tells them. But it doesn't matter. The best bit is true. Prue did open her eyes and she got better.

I was looking at those eyes now and wondering if Dad's theory was right and that all those concentrated hours and days of reading and music had helped turn Prue into a near-genius. It was hard to argue against it. Prue certainly loved her books and she was probably the only thirteen-year-old girl alive whose room could double as a Beatles shrine. On top of that, she knew every Beatles song ever recorded and could play most of them on three different instruments. In fact, with her mop of dark hair, she was even starting to look a bit like one of the Beatles!

"So what should we do now?" she said.

"Tell Mum."

That evening after tea, when Dad went to bed early feeling the effects of his all-night Beatle-fest, we went to Mum with our suspicions.

"Look, I know you're worried," she said as she handed me the last plate to dry. "Your father certainly hasn't been himself lately, I know that… He's got a lot on his mind… but it's not what you think."

Then she wiped her hands with a tea towel and took a deep breath. "It's got nothing to do with the Beatles," she said. "This is all about The Dugongs."

25.
The Return of
the Dugongs

"What, you mean Dad's old band?"

I didn't know much about The Dugongs except that they were formed when Dad was at uni and were only together for a few years before breaking up. That was about it. Of course Dad still strummed away on his guitar every now and then – he even taught me a few chords. But he never really talked much about his Dugong days. Mum neither.

Once I Googled their name, and apart from a million sites about marine creatures, the only reference I came up with was, 'The Dugongs: Rock band of the mid to late 1980s. Had strong local cult following but split when seemingly on the verge of wider success.'

"That's the one," Mum said. "When I first met your father at uni he was always going on about this band he was in. We used to talk sometimes before or after our American Lit tutorial. That's where we studied *Moby Dick*," she said with a wink at me.

"Yeah, yeah, I know *all* about that – let's just stick with The Dugongs, okay?"

"Well, your father and I became friendly and then one day he told me this band of his had a gig at uni. He asked if I'd like to come along to see them play, and I said yes."

"Were they any good?" Prue asked.

"The Dugongs?" Mum said, as if the answer was obvious. "They were *won*derful. Everybody loved them. After that first time I went to all their shows."

"Groupie chick, huh, Mum?"

"Fan, Prudence, fan," Mum said with an evil eye.

"But when you saw them play that first night, that's when you really fell for Dad, right?"

"No, not exactly... That's when I fell for Billy Mangan, actually."

"Who?"

"Billy Mangan. He was the drummer. Ron and Billy were best mates from school. They were very close. They wrote songs together – the next Lennon and McCartney, they reckoned. And Billy… Well, he was gorgeous. All the girls had their eyes on him, not just me."

Prue leaned in closer. "So… before you got together with Dad… did you and Billy…"

"Sorry, Prue, we're not in the Big Brother house. Billy was lovely, he really was. But so was your father… and *he* made me laugh."

"He made you laugh?" I said. "That's it? That's what did it for you?"

"Don't knock it," Mum said. "It sure beats the alternative."

"So what's all this got to do with Uncle Ray's email and Dad turning into one of the extras from *Dawn of the Dead*?"

"Well, Ray was their bass player."

Prue and I exchanged a look. "Uncle Ray was a *Dugong*?" I said.

"Of course. There was Ray on bass, Billy on drums, Leo McCrae on lead, and Ron on rhythm and main vocals. They had a *huge* following around the local venues – you've got no idea – and when Ron and Billy started to write more of their own stuff, they became even more popular. Some of the bands that were around at the same time went on to have hits in Australia and overseas, but back then they all played second fiddle to the Dugongs."

I asked the obvious question. "So how come The Dugongs never hit the big time?"

"Well, for a while there, it looked like they were going to. A friend of Ray's had a small recording studio in town and the band recorded an album of original songs."

"Wow, Dad made a CD?" Prue said.

"Vinyl and cassettes in those days. They only made a few hundred to begin with to sell at their gigs – but they were all gone in couple of weeks. Then a big record producer from Sydney got his hands on one and came to one of the shows. There was talk of a record contract and a national release." Mum paused and shook her head. "But it wasn't to be."

Prue beat me to the punch. "Why not?"

All of a sudden Mum seemed very tired. "Because Billy died in a car accident – the other driver was drunk. It happened... twenty years ago... today. Billy died, the band stopped playing, your father stopped writing songs and the big Sydney producer stopped pestering them about a contract. It all just... stopped."

"But didn't they ever try to get back together?"

"They talked about it, but it just seemed too hard – and painful, particularly for your father. Besides, Ron and I wanted to get married. We needed money... security. So he took that job with the insurance company. Just a temporary thing, really. But then there were bills to pay and then we had you... and Prue... And well, somehow he's been there ever since. The boys just drifted apart. Ray went into radio and Leo's been playing in pub bands in London."

Prue's brow wrinkled a little. "So today is the 20th anniversary of Billy's death," she said, "*and* I guess the twentieth anniversary of the death of The Dugongs as well. No wonder Dad has been so strange and sad. Do you think when he was listening to the Beatles last night that he was remembering how it was with The Dugongs and maybe... wondering what might have been?"

"I wouldn't be surprised," Mum said. "Billy and Ron always joked about The Dugongs being the new Beatles."

Prue nodded slowly. "So Uncle Ray's email... What was that all about?"

"A Dugongs twenty-year reunion concert."

Prue and I did one of those dopey double-takes.

"Yes, it knocked me for a six as well. Apparently Ray got a phone call recently from Leo. He'd been living in England for ages, but now he and his family have moved back here. Anyway, Ray and Leo got together and talked about the old days and came up with this idea of re-forming the band for a one-off performance. They've already dug up their old manager, although that doesn't thrill me too much, and they've lined up a possible replacement drummer – someone from one of the old bands they used to play with. The only missing piece in the jigsaw is your father, and that's what Ray's email was about – trying to convince him to agree."

"Is he going to do it?" I asked.

"Well, I'm sure that deep down he wants to, and maybe he needs to... But Billy's death hit Ron very hard. It might be too much to expect him to go back there. Anyway, he's meeting with Ray and Leo in town tomorrow, so I guess we'll just have to wait and see what happens."

"But what about you, Mum?" Prue asked. "How do you feel about it all? Are *you* ready for the return of The Dugongs?"

"Me?" Mum said with a weary smile. "I've been ready for twenty years."

26.
The Elephant of
Surprise

Apparently it took a bit of work, but my father finally said yes and The Dugongs' Twentieth Anniversary Reunion Concert was pencilled in for the end of the year – less than five months away.

Once that first shaky step had been taken, Dad stopped behaving like a fully paid-up member of the undead. Not that he magically returned to his old outgoing self or anything. In fact, at times he walked around looking as if he was about to have his first-ever bungee jump – off Sydney Harbour Bridge – at peak hour – naked. Other times he just looked sad. Like when he played his guitar, flicking through the old exercise book where he and Billy Mangan wrote down their songs. One night as I watched him I tried to imagine what it would be like to lose your best mate – to have to go through stuff alone. I didn't try to imagine that for very long.

I really wished that there was something I could do to help my father, but back at school I had my own worries – and for the first time that year they didn't involve either Barry Bagsley or Kelly Faulkner. No, this time the cause of my spiralling heart palpitations was the rapid approach of the debating season.

Our first meeting of the new term opened with a surprise announcement. Ignatius had joined the boarding school.

"You're a boarder now?" Razza said in astonishment. "Geez, Prindabel, I always suspected you were some kind of laboratory experiment gone wrong... but a *boarder*? Hey, wait on – don't you live just a couple of streets away from the school?"

"That's right."

"Then how come you're boarding? Has your family taken a restraining order out on you or something to stop you boring them to death?"

"No. My mother feels that boarding will be good for me. She says that relating more consistently and directly to boys my own age will accelerate my social development."

Razza studied Prindabel closely before delivering his verdict. "Tell her it's not working."

As you may have been able to detect, there was still some 'unresolved tension' between Razza and Ignatius over the 'Hot or what!' incident. Because of this, Scobie had decided that it might be wise if they didn't debate together for a while. It sounded like a fair enough plan, and it seemed to be working when Scobie, Razza and Bill easily won our first-round debate against Stonewall High. A couple of weeks later, Scobie, Prindabel and I followed it up by scoring a slim victory over Headly Grammar.

Of course Scobie was still the common ingredient in our success. He was as brilliant as ever as third speaker, polishing our case until it shone like gold and then stripping the opposition's bare until it looked like a rusty lump of scrap metal. This year, though, we didn't seem to rely on him quite as much. We were actually becoming a better team.

Because of this we went into our third-round match feeling pretty positive. This was despite the fact that Scobie and Prindabel were away on a special Science camp, leaving Razza, Bill and I to take on the team from St. Bartholomew's. As we waited for the result we were quietly confident we'd won. Unfortunately the adjudicator was loudly confident that we'd lost, and declared a two-point victory to St Bart's. Of course we were disappointed – especially Razza, who kept going on about being 'ripped off, big time'.

We knew it wasn't the end of the world, though. There was still one more first-round debate to go. If we could win that, it would give us three victories out of four, and that would be enough to send us through to the finals. For such a crucial debate we all agreed that it was time to select our strongest combination – Prindabel, Zorzotto and Scobie.

Although he lacked a little in the charisma department, Ignatius was certainly our best option as first speaker. He was organised and efficient and could outline our arguments clearly and precisely. Razza, as second speaker, could think on his feet, which was good for rebuttal. Whereas Prindabel was ordered and controlled, Razza had flair, personality and humour to carry him through. As third speaker, Scobie was... Well, Scobie was just Scobie. He made everyone else sound like dropouts from a pre-school remedial English class for Neanderthals.

Our opposition was going to be Strawberry Hill High. We knew they'd be tough, but we weren't panicking. After all, we had our best team on the case, didn't we? The topic was *That as a nation Australia pays too much attention to sport*. We were Affirmative – although as it turned out, some of us appeared slightly less affirmative than others.

"Man, what sort of a sicko dweeb came up with this topic, anyway? I mean, what've they got against sport? You know, this sounds like the sort of rubbish you'd come out with, Prindababble."

Also some of us still hadn't quite forgiven one of us for a certain less than favourable poetry review.

"Orazio, we've been through all this before," Scobie said with remarkable patience. "As I've pointed out already, we don't have to be anti-sport as such. Everything has its positives and negatives. It's just a debating topic, after all. But our *job* is to *focus* on the possible negative aspects of sport and show that Australia's *obsession* with it *can* lead to various problems and dangers."

"Problems and dangers? What problems and dangers?"

"Well, the kind of things we've been talking about in the last *three* meetings spring to mind. For example," Scobie said, reading from his detailed notes, "the encouragement of violence, aggression and gambling; the increasing incidence of serious injuries; the win-at-all-costs mentality that can result in the use of performance-enhancing drugs; the negative health effects of being a nation of spectators; the fact that too much of our taxes is being spent on sport and not enough in more important areas like health and scientific research; and the attitude that sports people are heroes, rather than people like scientists who, it could be argued, contribute vastly more to society."

Razza curled his lip at Ignatius. "Bet you came up with that last one, Prindabel. Who's your hero? The guy who designed the lab coat?"

Prindabel's thin lips became even thinner, but he didn't respond.

"Come on, Razz," I said, hoping to get us moving in the right direction, "we really need to focus here. The debate's next week. If we lose, that's it, we're gone."

"Yeah, well, we should have been through already, shouldn't we? Man, we were so mega-ripped off. I'm telling you guys, that adjudicator dude from the last round must have been blind not to see we were the much better team."

Prindabel raised his head and twisted his face into a question mark. "Blind? Don't you mean deaf? If he was blind he could still hear what both teams were saying and make a valid judgment, couldn't he? What you should have said was, 'He must have been deaf.' What you said doesn't make sense."

Razza glared across the table. "You know what I wish? I wish *you* were deaf, Prindabel. That way I wouldn't have to listen to you crapping on all the time."

"*Me* deaf? How would that stop you from hearing me? Wouldn't *you* have to be deaf? If I was deaf I could still speak, couldn't I? So you could still hear me, couldn't you? I might even know sign language, so I could even use that. Then if you didn't want to hear me *you'd* have to be deaf *and* blind."

Razza leaned forward and jabbed his pen at Ignatius. "You know what? I've seen backed-up toilets that weren't as full of crap as you."

"Well, when it comes to *crap*, we all know who won the Nobel Prize for that," Prindabel mumbled with a superior smile.

"Hey," Razza said thrusting a finger forward, "are you having another go at my poem? I told you before, Prindabel, you've totally got no idea, dude. Mr Guthrie said my poem was rigid and chronic. Tell him, Ishmael – go on, tell him what Guthrie said."

"Mr Guthrie said Razza's poem was rigid and chronic."

"See!"

"Yes, but what did he actually m—"

"Right, let's just forget all that," Scobie broke in. "It's not helping us get our case organised. Look, if we're going to be any chance of beating Strawberry Hill, we have to work as a team, and you know the old cliché, 'there's no *I* in team'."

"There's no *nerd* in team, either, so what's *he* doing here?" Razza said, jerking his thumb at Prindabel.

"Orazio, can we just forget Ignatius for a minute?"

"I'd like to forget him permanently."

"Look, last meeting, didn't we decide that *you* would concentrate on how our obsession with sport harms the individual and Ignatius would cover the negative effects sport obsession could have on groups and the nation as a whole?"

"Yeah… I suppose."

"So… Have you actually written up any of your arguments like you said you would?"

"Well, I haven't *quite* finished them."

"I've got mine right here, Scobie," Prindabel said, waving a bundle of paper in the air.

"Oh bravo, Tolstoy. Why don't you read it all aloud and we'll take bets on who'll be the first of us to die of boredom."

"So, Orazio… have you done *any*thing?"

"Look, Scobes… I was sick, all right? I was away on Monday, remember? You saw what I was like yesterday – well, on the weekend it was way worse. I was in bed most of the time. I couldn't talk 'cause my throat was so bad and I could hardly breathe. Man, it was like they were holding the world snot convention in my nose. What was I supposed to do?"

Prindabel held up his pen. "Here's a *rigid* thought. Maybe you could have recorded your experience for posterity by writing another one of your *chronic* poems. You could have called it 'Snot or What!'."

Razza flashed his eyes around the table at Bill, Scobie and me as each of us tried to stifle a laugh. Then he leaped up from his seat, pulled up his shirt and twisted from side to side, frantically examining his bare midriff.

"Ishmael, hurry for god's sake! Am I gonna be all right? Is there much damage? Will I pull through? Tell me. I can take it."

"Razza, what are you doing?"

"I can't believe it," Razza said, patting his stomach and feeling around to his back. "It's a miracle! You positive you can't see any rips or tears? I thought for sure my sides would have split when Prindabel came out with such a *hilarious* comment. Gee, Ignatius, can you warn us next time before you dump one of those absolute *gut*-buster howlers on us?" Razza sat back down after firing off a look of withering contempt at Ignatius.

"Orazio," Scobie said calmly, "you *really* do need to get your speech finished as soon as possible."

"Yeah, yeah, I know, okay. But I can't write everything

out word-for-word, right? I don't want to sound over-prepared and predictable. Unlike *some* people, I like to be flexible... spontaneous... *interesting* even. I like my speeches to have that... that elephant of surprise... You know what I mean?"

Prindabel leaned forward in his chair. "The *what* of surprise?"

"The *elephant* of surprise," Razza said in his *Play School* voice. "Gee, Prindabel, am – I – talk – ing – too – quick – ly – for – you?"

"Well, Orazio, I think you'll find that the correct expression is the *element* of surprise, not elephant."

"Element?" Razza scoffed. "Prindabel, I warned you about munching on too many computer chips, didn't I? Look, work it out for yourself. If you walked into a room, what do you think would give you the biggest surprise – to find an element there or an elephant? You can phone a friend if you like, Leonardo."

Prindabel held up his hands in despair. "How about we settle this straight away?"

"How?"

"*Elephantary*, my dear Zorzotto – we'll have a vote. Who thinks Orazio's correct and it's 'elephant of surprise'?" Prindabel checked each of us in turn. "Well now, *that's* a surprise," he said. "No elephants! Seems like the tribe has spoken, Orazio."

Razza looked at us as if we'd betrayed him. "Yeah, well maybe I was just being... you know... creative with language... Yeah, avoiding clichés like Miss Tarango always goes on about."

Scobie stepped in to save Razza further embarrassment. "Look, as we don't seem to be making much headway, perhaps it might be best if we finished up for now and meet again on Friday at lunchtime. Anyone have anything to add before we go?"

Bill and I shook our heads, but Ignatius nodded his thoughtfully. "Yes, you know what you should do?" he said to Razza. "First, you should take Scobie's notes and pick out all the arguments that apply to individuals and write them up fully. Then you should make sure you can tie everything to our team theme that 'too much of a good thing is harmful'. Then after you've done that, you should get on the internet and find the necessary facts and figures you'll need to use as supporting evidence. Oh, and you know what else you should do? You should make a photocopy of my speech. That way you won't overlap with my arguments and as well you'd see exactly how you should organise and set everything out. That's what you should do, Orazio."

Scobie then officially brought the meeting to an end, but only after Razza had taken just two words to explain exactly what *he* thought Ignatius should do.

27.
Tiny Pink Crop Circles

I wouldn't call the debate against Strawberry Hill a complete disaster. After all, nothing was destroyed and nobody died – not literally, anyway.

I guess the warning signs were there in our final two debating meetings. Razza and Prindabel refused to talk to each other except via insults and sarcastic asides and then they both argued (through Scobie) that the other's speech should be changed while stubbornly refusing to listen to any suggestion regarding their own.

The last meeting broke up when Ignatius accused Razza of being "living proof" that too much sport was harmful, since repeated heading of a football had obviously pulverised his brain. Razza fired back that the only way Prindabel would make it onto a sporting field was as a corner post – and even then he'd have to do extensive weight training to build himself up. At that point Scobie suggested that it might be better if Bill or I stepped into the team at the last minute. Both Ignatius and Razza agreed wholeheartedly as long as *they* weren't the one being replaced.

On the night of the debate, the room was packed. Strawberry Hill had a big crowd of supporters. They'd also dropped just the one debate, so it was do or die for them as well. I sat nervously in the audience with Mum and Prue, Bill and his parents, Mr Scobie, Mrs Zorzotto and a few younger St Daniel's boys from an earlier debate. Dad wasn't there because he was tied up with rehearsals and Miss Tarango couldn't make it either because she was with another of our teams at a different school. It was the first time in my life that I could remember being glad that Miss wasn't around. I had a bad feeling about this.

The two teams sat facing each other waiting for the adjudicator to signal the start. The girl and two boys from Strawberry Hill were crammed together, nodding and whispering and occasionally flicking nervously through their index cards. Across the room Razza, Scobie and Prindabel sat glumly like guests on the Jerry Springer Show who'd just been informed that they were all married to the same woman – and she was a man.

Finally, with a nod from the adjudicator, we were under way. The first speaker from Strawberry Hill was competent enough but I was still sure that Ignatius would at least be able to match him and that our case would hold up. When Prindabel rose to speak, however, it didn't take long for the cracks to appear.

The first sign of trouble came when Prindabel outlined our team argument. While he stated boldly that *he* as first speaker would "prove beyond a shadow of a doubt" and Scobie as third speaker would "convince with an overwhelming and watertight case", the best Ignatius could manage for Razza was "our second speaker will *attempt* to present *some* plausible arguments why you should believe him". I spotted a few frowns around the room. The biggest one was carved into Razza's face.

Don't worry, there was worse to come. The cracks widened alarmingly when Prindabel announced our theme. It seems that, without informing his teammates, he had decided to ever-so-subtly change the original theme from *Too much of a good thing is bad for you* to *Sport is for losers*. One of Scobie's eyebrows reared up like an exclamation mark. The opposition team began writing furiously. Across the room from them, and writing even more furiously, was Orazio Zorzotto.

But wait, Ignatius wasn't finished yet. Oh no. He had one last surprise for us all. It appeared that, in order to illustrate his arguments about the negative aspects of sport, he had decided it would be a good idea to base his evidence exclusively on football. It was as if no other sport existed. We heard about football drug cheats, football hooliganism and violence, serious injuries suffered by football players (including – Prindabel pointed out with a sympathetic glance at Razza – brain damage from excessive heading), outlandish incomes earned by football stars and finally, the pièce de résistance, the widespread bribery, corruption and match-fixing that Prindabel gleefully informed the audience was most rampant in Italian football clubs, particularly AC Milan.

When Ignatius returned to his chair, he briskly

tapped his index cards into alignment, placed them carefully on the desk and stared straight ahead. Beside him, James Scobie sat motionless like a small, pale, stone statue. On the other side of Scobie, Razza was leaning forward with his eyes boring into Prindabel as if he was trying to slice him in two with his X-ray vision. He stayed that way as the next speaker from Strawberry Hill delivered her speech.

Naturally their second speaker wasted no time in destroying Prindabel's theme and in pointing out the extremely narrow range of examples used to "prove" his arguments. Even before Razza had said a word, it was clear that the Negative team were ahead of us.

I knew we were in trouble, but I consoled myself with the knowledge that debating was more like a marathon than a sprint and therefore there was still plenty of time for us to catch up. Well, at least that's what I did think until Razza gave his speech. By the time he'd finished it was pretty clear to me that the opposition were already starting their final lap of the stadium while we were still four suburbs away asking tourists for directions.

Don't get me wrong. It wasn't that Razza's arguments

weren't convincing and passionate. They were. In fact in a lot of ways it was probably his most inspired performance. It was just unfortunate that he seemed to be more interested in debating Ignatius than the other team. As Strawberry Hill salivated with delight, Razza mounted a spirited defence of sport in general and football and AC Milan in particular. Just *occasionally* did he manage to drift almost accidentally over to our side of the debate. Like the time he acknowledged that an obsession with sport *might* have *some* harmful side effects, but then quickly pointed out (nodding towards Prindabel) that it was better than being "an uber nerd whose idea of exercise was blowing out the flame on a Bunsen burner".

When Razza returned to his chair, he briskly tapped his index cards into alignment, placed them carefully on the desk and stared straight ahead. Beside him James Scobie wrapped an elastic band around a big slab of his carefully prepared notes and dropped them into a bin beneath his desk. On the other side of Scobie, this time Prindabel leaned forward with his eyes boring into Razza as if he was trying to slice him in two with his X-ray vision.

As you can imagine, the final speaker for Strawberry Hill had a field day. Not content with driving a truck through the yawning holes in our arguments, he effortlessly piloted jumbo jets through sideways. By the time he'd finished, the Affirmative case as presented by our first two speakers was exposed as a broken-down heap of generalisations, inconsistencies, errors and contradictions.

The only problem that their third speaker seemed to be having was trying to fit all his excellent rebuttal points in before the bell. Of course, he could have saved a lot of time by just saying, "Ladies and gentlemen, I would like to point out two major flaws in the opposition's arguments – their first and second speakers. Thank you." That would have done juuuuust fine.

All eyes were now on Scobie. Since the end of Razza's speech he had been meticulously filling up blank index cards, point after point, with his loopy backhanded writing, and he didn't stop or raise his eyes until the chairperson called his name. Then he laid down his pen, straightened his cards and walked calmly to the front of the audience. "Chairperson, Ladies and Gentlemen," he said, adjusting his glasses on his small nose, "let me make it perfectly clear to you what we have heard here tonight..."

For the next five minutes there was only one show in town – and its star was James Scobie. I don't think anyone who was there will ever forget that speech. First Scobie began by salvaging any scraps of argument he could find from the pile of rubble left by the hand grenades that Ignatius and Razza had hurled at each other. Then he bound those bits together so cleverly that they appeared strong and solid. Piece by piece he painstakingly rebuilt our case until in the end even I was convinced I could see it standing up, although I knew there was absolutely no foundation to support it.

After that, Scobie turned his attention to the opposition and began a process of deconstruction and demolition. Calmly and clinically he exposed every design fault, every dodgy short cut, every structural weakness, every gap, every crack and every piece of shoddy workmanship. When he'd finished, what had once appeared safe and welcoming now had you reaching for the *Danger! Do Not Enter* sign.

The second warning bell sounded just as Scobie uttered his final words. The applause started then and followed him to his seat, and it continued as he sat gazing into the space between the teams. Even the adjudicator was shaking his head and clumping his hands together loudly. Through it all James Scobie sat motionless like a little Buddha framed by two sheepish faces. He was too exhausted to even raise a twitch.

In his summing up, the adjudicator said that Scobie's speech was by far the best he'd ever heard in a middle-school debate, and he followed it up by awarding it the highest marks he had given in nine years of adjudicating. But it still wasn't enough. We fell short by two points. There would be no finals glory for us this year.

After the chairperson officially closed the debate, Scobie was swamped. Even the Strawberry Hill supporters couldn't wait to congratulate him.

Mum told Scobie that he would be running the country one day. Scobie just smiled and said, "Thanks, Mrs Leseur – I don't know about that."

Then Mum headed off to catch up with Mrs Zorzotto, but for some strange reason, Scobie remained focused on the empty space where she had been. It took a second or two before I realised that he was looking at Prue.

"Oh… Scobie… This is Prue, my little sister. Prue,

this is James Scobie… and that's Razza… and Ignatius."

Prue was clutching a copy of *The Grapes of Wrath*. She smiled briefly at the other two then turned quickly back to Scobie. "You were just brilliant," she said with her eyes stretched wide in amazement, "and trust me, I know brilliant. Just a shame the rest of your *team* didn't show up," she said, firing some dagger eyes at Razza and Prindabel. "You could have won easily. But *your* speech… I still don't know how you did it… You were… fantastic."

Scobie cleared his throat then attempted to adjust his glasses, but only managed to accidentally knock them sideways so that they swung off one ear. As he fumbled them back into place his mouth twisted from side to side and neat patches of colour appeared on each of his cheeks like tiny pink crop circles.

"Thanks… It was… I umm… It ah… I ah… I umm," he said.

Standing beside me was the most brilliant speaker that St Daniel's Boys College was ever likely to produce – and something was turning his brain into mush.

Track 6:
All the Time

All the time
I've been looking at you
Can you see me?
Can you see me?

    All the time
    I've been trying to break through
    Won't you free me?
    Won't you free me?

        All the time
        I've been wishing I knew
        Will it be me?
        Will it be me?

            All the time
            I've been thinking of you
            All the time
            All the time

From The Dugongs: *Returned & Remastered*
Music & lyrics: W. Mangan and R. Leseur

28.
A Brain Snog

"Scobie and Prue?"

Razza nodded knowingly.

"Scobie... and Prue?"

"I'm telling you, man, he's got it and he's got it bad."

Razza and I both looked across the room to where Scobie sat quietly waiting for Miss Tarango to arrive for registration.

"Scobie and *Prue*?"

"You *were* there last night, weren't you? You heard him trying to speak to her, didn't you? And what about the look? You must have seen that. Just like I said – Game Over, man."

"But... Prue's just... a little *kid*."

"Little kid? She's only a year younger than you... and dude, have you studied her closely recently?"

"No!"

"Yeah well, maybe you should... I know I did last night," Razza said, then held up both hands when he saw the expression on my face. "Hey, it's what I do. Anyway, what I'm saying is, that if you had been paying a bit more attention you might've noticed that your *little* Prudles has undergone some interesting *redevelopments* and *expansions*, if you get my drift."

I did get his drift, but I wasn't sure if I really wanted to go where he was drifting.

"Besides, they reckon chicks mature faster than us guys... If you can believe *that*," Razza said as he bent a staple so one spike stuck up then placed it carefully on Donny Garbolo's chair. "*And* don't forget, she's a genius and everything, so that makes her technically even older. See, that's what I reckon it's all about – it's a meeting of the minds, man. So I wouldn't worry about the Scobster and the Pruester getting up to anything hot and heavy if I were you. They'd probably just want to do something like read encyclopedias or watch *Sale of the Century* or do algebra problems together. Be sort of like… a brain snog."

We were interrupted at that point by Donny Garbolo delivering an impressive spray of swear words as he extracted a staple from his backside.

Razza glared at him. "Do you mind keeping it down to a dull roar, pal? We're trying to have a serious conversation here."

Donny Garbolo's eyebrows hooded tightly together and he held up the staple. Razza turned to the boys around him and told them sternly that it was about time some people grew up. Donny looked at everyone as if they were in a police line-up, then checked his seat thoroughly before gently sitting down.

"So anyway… like I was saying before I was so rudely interrupted: Scobes is definitely gone, totally wasted. It's an open-and-shut case. Yep, it looks to me like Scobie baby has found his one Prue-love."

As Razza sniggered happily beside me, I saw the world I thought I knew crumbling away. What was going on? There was no one you could trust any more. First it was Barry Bagsley becoming almost human, and then it was my own father joining the legions of the living dead, and now logical, always-in-control, never-lost-for-words Scobie had warped into a babbling pile of hormones and was looking to brain-snog my little sister. It was getting scary.

A series of thumps from beside me broke my chain of thought. I looked across at Razza, who was drumming madly on his desk with his lips pushed forward, his eyes squeezed shut and his head flopping around as if his neck had turned to rubber. Occasionally he lashed out at an imaginary cymbal. I smiled to myself. It was good to know that at least *some* people would always be the same.

"Hey, nearly forgot," Razza said without missing a beat, "Billy Boy was talking about going to the cinema tomorrow to see the new *Star Warrior's Quest* flick. What's it called again?"

"*Star Warrior's Quest: The Final Hurdle.*"

"Yeah, sweet, *The Vinyl Girdle.*"

Yes, some people would never change.

"Anyway, you in?"

"Sure."

"Well, Bilbo's gonna ring me tonight to sort out the details, then I'll call you, okay?"

"Yeah, great."

"Cool!"

That night while my family were all sitting around the TV having our usual Friday night video marathon and fish and chips pig-out, I remembered what Razza had said about Prue and decided to observe her closely for myself. One thing I noticed straight away was that she seemed more interested in poring over last year's St Daniel's school magazine than watching the movie. Something else was pretty obvious as well – two things, really. I guess maybe Razza was right – maybe my little sister Prue wasn't that little any more.

I shifted my attention from Prue to Dad. Normally he would be cracking jokes about whatever was happening on the TV or making up his own dialogue for the characters on the screen. Not tonight. Tonight he was just chewing slowly on a chip and staring into space like he was tuned in to an entirely different programme. Mum wasn't much better.

What was happening to everyone?

I can tell you, it was a relief when the phone finally rang. "That'll be for me," I said, hurdling over the coffee table and heading for the hallway. I was glad to get out of there. I was looking forward to speaking with the one person I knew would never go all weird on me.

I yanked up the receiver, blurted out, "Ishmael here," and waited for Razza's unmistakable rapid-fire delivery to barrel down the line.

"Ishmael?" a soft voice replied. "Hi, it's Kelly Faulkner."

29.
Scope to Grope

"Rigid, dude! Now do you believe me? She's pining for you, man! Hey, was she naked again?"

I'd only just finished talking to Kelly Faulkner when Razza rang.

"No, she wasn't naked, okay?"

"Then tell me *exactly* what she said."

"She said her debating team were through to the finals. She said that they'd heard about us being knocked out and she wanted to know if both of us could help them with their preparation for the Secret Topic round next term because we'd been through it all last year. She said maybe we could meet at Sally's house on the second weekend of the break. Oh, and she also said that Sally's father found a cordial bottle stuck somewhere up the back of the pool filter."

"Awesome! I never doubted you for a second, dude. You know what this means, don't you? She wants you, man! She wants you!"

As excited as I was to get a phone call from Kelly, after the disaster of the party I was determined not to read too much into it.

"Razz, it was about debating."

"About debating? About debating? Dude, I don't believe you. You're not just a *glass half-empty* sort of a guy, are you? You're more a *glass half-empty and there's probably a dead cockroach on the bottom* sort of a guy. Geez, Ishmael, she rang you up. Do you hear what I'm saying? She rang you. What does she have to do, man – knock you over the head with a club and drag you into a cave? Look, think about it – first she invites you to Sally's party and *now* she's inviting you to help out with debating. Could it be any more obvious? Mate, it's *not* about debating. The debating thing's just for show. It's just a front, a fraud, a cover-up. It's all about you and her getting it on."

"You don't know that for sure. She just might

really want to win the debate."

"Okay, okay, let's just say that's true. Then explain to me why, of all people, she's asking us for help? Look, no offence, dude, but neither of us exactly qualifies as the Michael Jordan of debating, do we?"

"But what about our Secret Topic experience?"

"What, you mean our *losing* experience?"

"But we did all right. We *almost* won. Besides, it doesn't matter. We still went through it all. We can still tell them what it's like, can't we?"

"Yeah maybe, but if *you* really wanted help with debating who would *you* go to?"

That was simple. "Scobie."

"Of course you would. Everyone knows Scobie is the best debater in the entire comp by a mile, right? Sally even said at her party that they'd heard all about him from the other teams. So here's my question. Did Kelly seem super keen for Scobie to come along?"

"Well… no… not really. She mainly just talked about you and me… but…"

"Ladies and gentlemen of the jury, I rest my case."

"But maybe she's just assuming that he'll come along too."

"Yeah, maybe she is. *But* if it was all about debating, if she *really* just wanted to win and that's all, then she'd make sure Scobie was going to be there, wouldn't she? Scobie would be priority numero uno. But dude, I'm telling you, she hasn't got her eye on Scobie – she's after *you*."

I wanted to believe Razza. I really did, but it just didn't seem possible. Kelly Faulkner wanting me? It was about as likely as Snow White wanting Dopey.

"Trust me, man – have I ever been wrong before?"

That was simple too. "Yeah, heaps of times."

"But recently?"

"U-huh – you said Bagsley would never hit anyone at school, then he punched my lights out, right in the middle of my own form room."

"Well, if you're gonna pick up on every minor detail, I'm outta here. But you'll see, man. Kelly's got her eyes on you for *something*, all right, but it ain't debating."

The following week, despite Razza's protests, I told the rest of the team about Kelly's phone call and asked if any of them wanted to come. Bill didn't seem that keen and Prindabel was going to be away with his family somewhere. Scobie was free though, and I convinced him to join us so at least we would have one person who really knew what he was talking about.

Razza didn't seem that concerned about the extra company. "Yeah, you know it might be good to have the Scobster there. He'll be a distraction for the other chicks."

Then he nudged me in the ribs and wiggled his eyebrows up and down. "That'll give you and the Big K more scope to grope."

30.
Carpet Dinkum – Squeeze the Day

We decided to meet at my house before we went to Sally's. Mum was going to drive us over and pick us up in the afternoon. Razza and Scobie arrived early.

"So this is your room, eh, Ishmael? This is where all the action happens, is it? The Leseur lair. Man, it's pretty wild." (Because you can't see my room, it might surprise you to know that Razza was actually being sarcastic here.)

I guess I hadn't really thought about it much before, but I had to admit, my room was pretty plain. For a starter, the walls were mainly bare except for an embarrassing old poster of *Finding Nemo* that Dad had put up for me when I was a kid. Razza was examining it closely.

"Geez, I hope they find that little fella soon. How long has it been now?"

I sat down on the bed beside Scobie as Razza continued his tour. He moved to the corner of the room and a row of plastic boxes stuffed full of old toys that I hadn't touched for years. He reached in and pulled out a floppy Snoopy doll. "Wicked," he said before dropping it back and completing one last sweeping inspection.

"I guess your parents are worried sick about you, are they, dude? You know, terrified about you being caught up in heavy metal, satanic worship, hard drugs and stuff?"

I didn't respond. I was just glad I'd convinced Mum to get rid of my Thomas the Tank Engine eiderdown last year.

Then Razza picked something off the shelves above my desk. "Hey, what's this, man?" He was holding up a Dugongs cassette.

"That's my dad's band – from when he was at uni."

"All right! Your dad was in a band. Cool! And they recorded an album? Awesome! What's it like – any good?"

"Yeah, not bad. I like it."

I did too. A couple of months ago Mum, Prue and I had watched as Dad cut open a sealed box he'd dug from a cupboard in the back room. Inside were the leftover cassettes and vinyl albums of The Dugongs' first and only recording. I'd heard Dad play songs at home before, but it was strange to see a thin version of him on the cover of an album along with the rest of the band and stranger still to imagine him leaping around on stage. The way he'd been since he agreed to do the reunion thing – sort of quiet and scared – made me wonder if he still had it in him. I guess he was wondering the same thing.

"Man, that is so cool," Razza said, flipping over the cassette in his hand. "'Cept for the name, of course. What is a *dugong*, anyway? Some kind of bug or moth, isn't it?"

"That would be your bogong," Scobie said. "*Agrotis infusa* – a small moth from the Noctuidae family – follows a mass migration in spring."

Razza and I took part in a communal gawk.

Scobie blinked back at us.

"My father's an entomologist. It's really quite a well-known moth."

"I'll take your word for it. So what's a dugong, then?"

"Ah, that would be your sea cow," I said, "a member of the manatee family, although strangely enough more closely related to the elephant. Lives in the sea, grazes on sea grass, has poor eyesight but excellent hearing. Looks a bit like a bloated seal."

Razza transferred his gawk to me. "Don't tell me – your father is a marine biologist. Right?"

"Wrong – insurance salesman. I picked up that stuff Googling the band's name."

"So let's see… Your father's band is named after some fat, blind, underwater, elephanty-type thing that pigs out on sea grass." Razza shook his head. "Rock 'n' roll, man."

"I think there might have been dugongs or something around where he grew up. Anyway, as far as band names go, it's the 'The' bit that's important."

"The 'The' bit?"

"Yeah, Dad's always going on about how all the really big groups in the past were called the something. You know, like *the* Beatles, *the* Rolling Stones…"

"*The* Wiggles," Razza suggested. "So tell me about *The Dugongs*," he said, holding up the cassette. "What happened to them?"

So I told Razza and Scobie all about the band and the big reunion concert at the end of the year. When I'd finished Razza tapped the cassette against his hand. "Any chance I can borrow this and check them out?"

"Sure."

"Awesome, dude, thanks," Razza said as he stuffed the tape in his jacket pocket. Then, having finished his tour of my room, he turned his attention to Scobie, who was sitting on the bed with his feet dangling a few centimetres above the carpet. "Hey, Scobie baby, you're looking pretty sharp today, dude. Is that a new shirt, by any chance? Haven't made a *special* effort for any reason, have we?"

Scobie looked up at Razza blankly.

"Wouldn't have anything to do with someone's hot sister, would it?"

Again Scobie said nothing.

"Speaking of hot sisters, where *is* Prue?"

"Out shopping with Mum – they should be back soon."

"Well Scobes, my man, do you want my advice?"

"Strangely enough, no," Scobie said.

This didn't surprise me, because even though many people regularly *received* Razza's advice, I'd never yet met anyone who had actually *wanted* or *asked* for it. Of course, this never seemed to bother Razza in the slightest.

"What you gotta do, man, is grab the moment. You know what I mean? Like in that *Deadly Poets* flick Miss showed us in English where that teacher dude kept saying *Carpet dinkum, squeeze the day*. So here's what you gotta do if you want to win Prue. You gotta tell her how hot and smokin' she is, okay? Chicks love compliments, so lay it on thick. Oh… and it's really important to be sincere, even if you don't mean it."

Scobie's mouth curled from one side to the other then stretched downwards, but he remained silent.

"Please yourself. Just trying to help." With that, Razza began digging through the toy boxes while singing just loud enough for Scobie to hear, *You're just too good to be true. Can't take my eyes offa Prue. She feels like heaven to touch. Scobes wants to hold her soooooo much* until something more important distracted him. "Hey, cool! Pirate Lego!"

Ten minutes later Razza was happily building a pretty impressive pirate island and Scobie was flicking through Dad's old copy of *Moby Dick* when Prue burst into the room.

"Hey Ishy, check out the earrings Mum bought me! Aren't they…" She stopped in her tracks when she spotted Razza and Scobie. "Oops… sorry."

"Hi, Prudles," Razza said with a cheesy grin. "Remember me, Razza? From the debating?"

"Of course." Prue smiled back sweetly. "Which side were you on again? It was so hard to tell."

Razza threw up his hands. "Man, you make one *little* mistake and they make you pay for it for the rest of your life."

Prue laughed then tucked her hair behind her ears. I noticed something else about Prue then as she stood in front of Scobie in a little tank top and a pair of checked shorts – she wasn't quite as straight up and down as she used to be.

"Hi, James," she said in a syrupy kind of voice (another recent development).

Scobie shot back a Halloween pumpkin grin and mumbled like he had a gob full of superglue.

Prue fiddled with her earlobe. "Well… I suppose I'd better get out of your way. I've got things to do… you know… books to read and guinea pigs to feed."

But Razza jumped in before she could move.

"So Prue, you got new earrings, eh? Sweet! Give us a look. Man, they're *so* cool on you. What d'ya reckon, Scobes? Don't you think Prue's new earrings are cool? Don't you think they make her look *beautiful?*"

All eyes fell on Scobie, who was concentrating hard on Razza. Then he turned stiffly to face my little sister. She smiled at him then looked away quickly. Scobie said nothing. Razza gave a nervous laugh.

"Well, Scobes, come on, don't keep us waiting. Don't you reckon Prue's new earrings make her look beautiful?"

Scobie blinked. "Not really... no," he said.

Razza's eyes exploded like mushroom clouds and Prue's smile melted away like the polar ice caps.

"Wh... what? Hey he's... he's just kiddin'," Razza said, spinning around to Prue. "The old Scobster's *always* joking. Man, he really slays me sometimes! Come on, dude," he said turning back to face Scobie, "quit jerking us around and be serious for once, will ya? Tell us the *truth* now." Then Razza spoke slowly and deliberately as if he were interrogating a hostile witness. "Don't you think... that the earrings... make Prue... look beautiful?"

Scobie regarded Razza calmly. "No. No, I don't think... that the earrings... make Prue... look beautiful."

Razza had his back to Prue, but from the bed I could see his mouth fall open and his eyes glaze over in disbelief. I looked at my sister. Her expression was a bit like Razza's, only with a little less disbelief and more hurt. I couldn't believe what I was hearing either.

But Scobie wasn't finished. I guess we all should have known that he would always have the final word.

"No," he said, "I think... that *Prue*... makes *them* look beautiful."

What followed was a few seconds of absolute silence before Prue gave a sort of half-cough, half-giggle and pointed back over her shoulder.

"Well, I um... I should um... I have to... you know... do that um... stuff I have to do... you know... book the guinea pigs and read the feeds."

She stared blankly ahead for a moment then backed her way awkwardly out the door. Almost immediately she reappeared. "I got that a little confused just then," she said with great composure. "Of course what I *meant* to say was that I had to feed the books and read the guinea pigs."

Then she smiled, frowned, blushed, giggled and blushed again in rapid succession before spinning round and bounding down the stairs.

We all remained motionless like three slightly overdressed crash-test dummies.

Then Razza drifted across the room like a sleepwalker and sat down beside me on the bed. For a moment or two he looked up at Scobie in silent awe. Finally he spoke. "Bow your head, Ishmael," he whispered. "We are in the presence of greatness."

31.
The Break-and-enter Chick

When we arrived at the Nofkes' house, Sally said that three of the other girls were running late. I didn't mind. Kelly was there and she had her hair pulled back in a little ponytail. She looked so cute it was like torture.

After we introduced Scobie, we were taken through to the lounge room, where Sally's little sister Sophie was sitting on the floor clutching a storybook. Beside her was a slightly older boy playing with a Nintendo DS. Sophie looked up at me and her face darkened. I don't think she had quite forgiven me for implicating her in the Pool Piddle fiasco.

"James, this is my little sister Sophie and my little brother Jeremy. You guys already met Ishmael and Razza at my party. Now I'm afraid you'll both have to move out now – we have to work on our debate."

Sophie's mouth dropped open like an M&M dispenser. "But you gotta wead me a story. You said."

"I know, Soph, but I can't now. We've got work to do and Kelly and I have to finish making sandwiches. Anyway, Mum and Dad will be back soon, so maybe you could ask one of them."

"But I want you to wead it. You said. You pwomised!"

"How about if I read you lots of stories tonight, okay?"

"But you pwomised to wead me a story *now*!"

Sally looked flustered. "Soph, sweetie… look…"

"I'll wead you a story."

Everyone looked at Razza.

"No, look, you don't have to do that," Sally said.

"I don't mind, really. I'll read the story while you guys make the sandwiches."

"I don't think you know what you're letting yourself in for. Sophie's pretty… picky. She knows her favourite stories off by heart. She'll catch you out if you try to skip anything."

"That's cool. No problem. I got a million little cousins. I was born to read!"

Sally knelt down beside her little sister. "What do you say, Soph? Would it be okay if Razza read your story instead?"

Sophie looked up doubtfully at Razza. "I know my ABC," she said.

"Just ABC? That's nothing," Razza countered, "once I got all the way through to K without even looking!"

Sally smothered a smile with her hand. Kelly rolled her beautiful eyes. Sophie just stared at Razza for a while then stood up and climbed onto the couch.

"Cool!" Razza said. "What're we reading?"

Sophie held up the book. It was *Goldilocks and the Three Bears*. "Awesome – the break-and-enter chick! One of the classics!"

"Well, if you guys are all right by yourselves for the moment, Kel and I will finish getting the food organised."

We were, so the girls headed for the kitchen and Scobie and I sat down on the two lounge chairs facing Razza and Sophie.

"You wanna join in?" Razza asked Jeremy, who curled

up his lip and looked insulted at the suggestion that he might consider listening to a reading of *Goldilocks*.

"Please yourself, little dude. Okay then, let's get this show on the road. And don't worry, Soph. Reading is my life. I have everything under control."

Razza took the book from Sophie, winked at her and opened it confidently. Then he squinted at the page in front of him as a puzzled expression invaded his face. Finally he drew in a sharp breath and slapped himself on the forehead with an open palm. "Of course," he said with a tsk-ing sound before rotating the book 180 degrees so that it was right way up.

Sophie looked on in horror. Jeremy peeked over the top of his Nintendo DS.

Razza continued. "Right, here we go. You ready? Let's see," he said, clearing his throat loudly, "*The Adventures of Pinkilocks and the Three...*"

"*No-o-o-o-o!*"

Sophie looked shocked.

"What's up?"

"You said *Pinkilocks*. It's not *Pinki*locks. It's *Goldi*locks."

"You sure?" Razza said, holding the book close to

his eyes. "Oh yeah… Yeah, you're right… There it is… Goldilocks. Must have been the light – plus being slightly colour blind doesn't help. Sorry about that, chief. No more mistakes from here on."

Scobie and I exchanged a look. Jeremy lowered his Nintendo DS to his lap. Sophie watched Razza like he was a dangerous criminal.

"Okay. Let's make a fresh start and get it right. Everyone's entitled to one mistake." There was more exaggerated throat clearing and then… *"The Adventures of Goldilocks… and the Three Beers."*

"Bears!" Sophie screamed at him.

"Where?" Razza screamed back as he leapt off the couch.

Ignoring her brother, who was chuckling, Sophie jabbed her finger at the page. "In the *story*. It's three *bears*, not *beers*. You got it wrong again."

"Phew, that's a relief," Razza said, climbing back beside Sophie. "I thought we were under grizzly attack. Anyway, good thing it isn't beers. This chick is way too young to drink. Just remember, Soph – Uncle Razz says if you drink and break into a bear's home, then you're an idiot, okay?"

Jeremy laughed out loud and bottomed his way across the carpet, but Sophie folded her arms tightly across her chest and clamped her brow into a fierce frown. "Do it poply."

Razza held up his hands. "Sorry, the pressure just got to me and I admit it... I choked. I'll get it right... I pwomise."

Sophie's face remained set hard.

Razza gave Jeremy a terrified look and pretended to chew his nails. Then he tried to pick up the book, but his hands were shaking so much he had to press it flat on his lap. Jeremy rolled back on the floor holding his stomach. Razza took a deep breath and blew out slowly like he was preparing for a world-record attempt in the clean and jerk. He began to read.

"The Adventures of... *Goldi*locks..."

Razza raised his eyebrows at Sophie, who nodded once. "... and the Three... *Bears*."

Razza checked again and Sophie nodded a second time. Razza smiled and ploughed on confidently. "Twice upon a time there lived a little girl called Goldilocks. One day..."

"*No-o-o-o-o-o-o-!*" Sophie let out a bellow that

towards the end warbled into a giggle. "It's once – once upon a time, not *twice*. You said *twice*!"

"Only once?" Razza said in disgust. "Man, you fork out big money for these books and they only give you a 'once'. What a rip-off! It's daylight robbery. I've got a good mind to…" Then Razza stopped and turned to Sophie, who was desperately trying to maintain her hard schoolteacher scowl. He smiled sheepishly. "Poply?" he asked.

"Poply," Sophie replied sternly but with a slight quiver on the edges of her little down-turned mouth.

Razza pushed out his lips and nodded. "Okay… Poply. *Once* upon a time there lived a little girl called Goldilocks. One day when she was walking in the forest, she came across a neat little cottage. Inside the cottage lived three bears." Razza paused proudly and looked for approval from Sophie, who smiled warily. Razza went back to the story.

"There was… *Poppa* Bear…"

He glanced up at Sophie and Jeremy.

"There was… *Momma* Bear…"

He glanced up again.

"And there was…"

Razza's eyes flicked around the room then settled back on the page.

"… mutant-two-headed-blood-sucking-spew-chucking -alien-baby bear!"

Sophie shrieked and cackled with laughter all at the same time. Jeremy cheered and leaped up onto the couch, where he bounced around shouting, "Yay! Mutant-blood-sucking-baby bear! Mutant-blood-sucking-baby bear!"

At this point Kelly and Sally stuck their heads around the doorway.

"What's going on?" Sally said. "Is someone being murdered in here?"

"Just a bit of quiet reflective reading," Razza said innocently.

"Yeah, we're reading Pinkilocks and the three blood-sucking alien bears!" Jeremy shouted.

"Really? Well I'm afraid you guys will have to run along soon. Razza's got to help us with debating."

"No!" Sophie said. "Wazzie's gotta stay here with us. He's got to finish the story." To emphasise the point she wriggled onto Razza's lap and locked his arms together as if she was strapping herself in for a roller coaster ride.

"Yeah," Jeremy added, jumping on Razza's back and grabbing him around the neck, "Razzie's gotta stay here with us."

Razza tilted his head to one side and smiled helplessly. "What can I do? I'm a prisoner in the system."

"All right, all right," Sally relented with a smile, "I can see that I'm outvoted. You can finish the story. But that's it, you guys, okay? One story and then we've got work to do."

Both Sophie and Jeremy cheered. "Wead, Wazzie," Sophie said.

"Poply?" Razza asked.

Sophie thought for a moment then clamped her mouth shut and shook her blonde curls furiously.

"Wicked!" Razza said, and he and Jeremy shared a high five. "Now where were we?"

While he searched for the place, Jeremy burrowed under his arm to get closer to the action.

"Here we are. Cool! One of my fave bits is coming up – Goldilocks and the snot-infested porridge."

"Wicked!" Jeremy said. Sophie cheered and slid her arm around Razza's neck.

As I watched the three of them on the couch I became aware of a sort of humming, sighing sound coming from the doorway. I turned around to see both girls watching Razza intently. Kelly was smiling, but Sally almost looked as if she was in pain.

"That is soooooooooooo sweeeeeeeeeeet!" she purred while she gazed at Razza in a strange, misty, dreamy sort of way.

Game Over, man.

32.
The Freakiest, Most Bizarre Thing

The freakiest, most bizarre thing happened at Sally's house that afternoon. It was this: nothing freaky or bizarre actually happened.

What I mean is, I wasn't accused of turning the pool into a urinal, I didn't go to the bathroom and come back with five metres of toilet paper trailing from my shorts or my underpants on the outside, I didn't accidentally purée the family budgie in the blender, I didn't even mistake the ashes of Sally's dead grandmother for a jar of pepper and sprinkle her over my lunch. As unbelievable as it might seem, I didn't do any of the things that a long-term sufferer of Ishmael Leseur's

Syndrome could be expected to do. In fact, I'm pretty sure I behaved like a normal person and, just as amazingly, I think we actually helped Kelly and her team with their debate.

Not long after Razza finished reading *Goldilocks*, the other three Lourdes girls turned up and we got down to work. Razza and I (mainly Razza) told them all about last year's short preparation debate and how Bill almost won it for us, then Scobie took over and gave the girls some great tips on how to divide up their time, what to bring along on the night and what kind of topics to expect. He even went through a practice debate preparation using the hour time limit.

But the best part of the day was later, when we ate and I got to sit next to Kelly after Razza deliberately bulldozed me into the spare chair beside her. Suddenly I found myself close enough to Kelly Faulkner to smell the rose scent of her perfume; close enough to make out tiny flecks of gold in her ice-blue eyes; close enough for her to accidentally brush her arm against mine while she was talking and close enough even to start dreaming that we could be close in more ways than just space.

All afternoon we just talked and laughed. Everything

seemed so easy. Razza had everyone in hysterics, especially Sally, and I don't think any of the girls had ever met anyone quite like Scobie before. Even I managed to contribute something after someone said I had an interesting name and I gave in to pressure from Razza (who else?) and told them how I ended up being called Ishmael.

Then everyone got in on the act. Razza said he was named after his great, great grandfather Orazio who was a pig farmer in Italy. Two of the other girls, Phoebe and Susan, said they were named after relatives as well. Sally told us that she got her name because her mother's favourite movie was *When Harry Met Sally*. Scobie didn't really know how his name came about and Gossamer thought hers was probably made up.

When it came to Kelly's turn she said it was "a bit embarrassing" but her parents named her after Princess Grace of Monaco, who was a Hollywood actor called Grace Kelly before she married a prince. "So my full name is actually *Kelly Grace Faulkner*," she said with a crooked smile. It sounded just perfect to me.

I found out some other things about Kelly Faulkner that day, like when Sally mentioned about her wanting to be a writer. "She's really brilliant," Sally said. "We'll all end up in a Kelly Faulkner best-seller one day, you wait."

Kelly just shook her head shyly.

"It's true," Phoebe added. "She never goes anywhere without her diary, and she's always scribbling away in it. So you better watch what you say. I'd hate to think what you've written about me in there, Kel."

Razza's eyes lit up. "Hey, that's just like Ishmael. He wrote this humongous journal thingo last year. Maybe you two should get together. You know... to compare notes and stuff. You could be, like, pen pals or something."

A few laughs and comments bounced around the table. I couldn't tell you what Kelly was doing, because at the time I felt like someone had slam-dunked my heart, and my face was sizzling like deep-fried chicken. "It was nothing," I mumbled, and thankfully the conversation soon moved on.

We talked like that for over an hour, until a storm began to move in and the wind started to blow rain on to the deck.

"This is all Kelly's fault," Sally said as we cleared up the table and headed for cover.

"Kelly's fault? How come?" Razza asked.

"Well, *I* organised the place and she was in charge of the weather. She's got connections, you know. People in high places."

Kelly gave a pained smile and sighed heavily. "My dad – he works in the weather bureau. He's the head guy. So of course, every time it rains when it shouldn't or it's too cold or too windy or too hot or too something, my so-called *friends* blame me. Now, does that seem fair to you? Just because I'm the daughter of a weatherman – does it?"

She was asking me. "No... No way."

"See!" Kelly said, pointing at Sally and the other girls, "Ishmael's on my side. Ishmael will defend me."

I was and I would – to the death.

Not long after that Mum arrived to pick us up and just about the most perfect afternoon of my life came to an end.

That night as I lay in bed listening to the rain, I couldn't stop my imagination from taking over. I saw myself alone with Kelly Faulkner, looking into her ice-blue eyes and telling her everything I had kept secret for so long. Then I pictured Kelly gazing at me and saying my name and moving towards me in slow motion until she was so close that I could feel her breath on my lips and then... and then... And then everything blurred and warped into nothingness. I guess there must be some things too impossible even for dreaming. But it still didn't stop me from wishing and praying that somehow a miracle would happen and one day Kelly Faulkner would look deep into my eyes and say my name with real passion.

And guess what? My fairy godmother must have been listening in.

Track 7:
Bad Day for Angels

It was a morning
When the sun kissed the sky
And you were yawning
As I watched you walk by
Then you smiled at me
And I heard you say
Looks like it's gonna be
A beautiful day

But sometimes it's so hard to know
Just which way the world will go

Chorus
It was a bad day for angels
A bad day for putting on wings
A bad day for angels
And magical things
A bad day for angels
Don't look in the sky
A bad day for angels
A bad day to fly

From The Dugongs: *Returned & Remastered*
Music & lyrics: W. Mangan and R. Leseur

33.
A Win, Win, Win, Win Situation

Back at school Razza was pretty hyped up, even by his standards.

"Man, I told you. I told you! Did I tell you or what? You and Kelly, dude – it's so on. She digs you, man. There's no stopping you now. You are cookin' big time, dude. You are cooooooooook – in'!"

I was determined not to let Razza get my hopes up too high. The afternoon at Sally's had been great, but on the other hand, nothing really happened between us and as far as I knew Brad was still lurking around somewhere. Still, even *I* had to admit, things were certainly looking up.

"Yeah, well I don't know about that, but what about you?" I said, hoping to take some pressure off myself. "You and Sally."

Razza gave me one of his rare serious looks. "Sally rocks, man. Sally's… brilliant. But that's the problem… I told you before, man. I know my limits and she's way out of bounds for me."

"Razz, you're wrong. You didn't see her looking at you when you were reading that story. She gave you the face – the Game Over face. She said you were sweet – I heard her."

"Probably talking about the ankle biters."

"But what about the way she was laughing at all your jokes? She almost choked at one stage."

"Someone laughing at you and someone liking you are not necessarily the same thing, man." Then he smiled. "Anyway, I'm on to you, dude, so quit trying to sidetrack me. This is about you and Kelly Faulkner getting together. That is my quest and I won't be denied. Onwards and upwards!"

Two weeks later, when the girls won their short preparation final, Razza and I were there to congratulate them and to arrange another get-together, this time at

Kelly's house, to help prepare for the big semi-final.

Because they knew the topic in advance for this one, back at school Razza and I, with help from Scobie, Bill and Prindabel, put together a bunch of arguments that we thought their opposition might use against them. At one point Razza turned to me with a smirk. "You know, I wonder why Kelly didn't just ask us to email these arguments to her? Would have been much easier and quicker than us going all the way over to her place, don't you reckon? Strange."

I was thinking about what to say to that when he jabbed me in the ribs. "You are *so* in, dude!"

On the day itself, it was just Razza and me who went along to Kelly's. Scobie couldn't make it because he was going with his father to some insect and bug convention and neither Bill nor Ignatius were interested. As it turned out, Sally and Kelly were alone as well. When we moved inside Razza secretly gave me the old bouncing eyebrows. I knew exactly what he meant.

For most of the day everything seemed perfect again. We met Kelly's parents, who were really nice, and they said it was wonderful to meet me because they knew all about how I tried to stop Barry Bagsley and his mates from bullying their son Marty. Then of course Razza had to embarrass me by saying, "Don't worry – he does that kind of stuff *all* the time," but I guess I didn't mind too much.

After that we went with the girls to a big study area downstairs and for the next couple of hours we actually focused on the debate, developing counter arguments and possible rebuttal points. The rest of the day the four of us sat around under the pergola in the garden talking, joking and swapping stories about school, and stuff like our favourite movies and most embarrassing moments (I had a big backlog of material here) and a million other things. Razza even made me tell them all about Dad and The Dugongs' reunion concert.

I was hoping the day would never have to end – that somehow the rest of my life could be spent sitting under that pergola. Eventually though, Mum called on the mobile saying she was on her way to pick us up and Razza and I went down to the study to collect our rucksacks.

As soon as we were alone Razza started. "You and Kelly are really hitting it off, man. I reckon it's time to bring out the big artillery."

Now I was worried. "Big artillery? What are you talking about?"

"This… Ta! Da!" Razza said, whipping something from the side pocket of his rucksack and holding it in front of my nose.

It was the poem. The old 'Hot or what!'. It was like having a corpse leap out at you from a coffin. Razza hadn't even mentioned it for over a month, but here it was, resurrected in a fancy font on a small rectangle of paper with the words *To Kelly* added at the top. To give Razza some credit, it *looked* a lot better. Unfortunately it still *sounded* the same.

"Razz, how many times do I have to tell you? There is no way I'm giving *that* to Kelly. No way."

"Look, man, maybe you were right to say that when you'd hardly spoken to her, but not now. Now look at you two, eh? Rapping and laughing together. Don'tcha see? Now it's different – now's the time to strike. She's starting to fall for you, man, and this poem could be just the thing to really push her over the edge!"

I couldn't argue with that.

"Look… I know you're only trying to help… but it's not going to happen, okay? Remember that stuff

Mr Guthrie said about it having to come from me? Well, I think that's true. Anyway, I'm not going do anything until I know for sure what Kelly really thinks of me."

"Dude, what more proof do you want? What about at Sally's? What about today?"

"What about Brad? Maybe she's just being friendly and nice… like she is to everyone."

Razza groaned as I held out the poem for him to take back. "No, keep it, man, keep it," he said, waving a hand at me and walking away, "just in case some miracle happens and you change your mind."

I was about to shove the poem in my pocket when Razza's voice returned in a strange whisper. "Hey… Check this out."

When I looked up he was holding a red-velvety-covered book. "You know what *this* is, don't you? It's Kelly's diary, man – you know, the one Sally told us about? Well, this is it. I saw her with it when we first got here."

I shot a hasty look at the door. "Razz, what're you doing? Put it down."

"It's all right. Don't panic, man."

"Razz, it's not all right. What happens if Kelly comes in and sees you with her diary? Can you just put it down... please!"

Razza gasped in exaggerated horror and placed the diary slowly back on the desk as if it were nitroglycerine.

"There – you happy?"

I nodded and waited for my heart to stop bouncing around like a Lotto ball in my chest.

"Look," Razza said calmly, "didn't you just say you wanted to know what Kelly really thought about you? Well... I bet the answer is right here." He placed his hand on top of the diary and flicked the pages casually with his thumb.

I couldn't believe what I was hearing.

"You're not serious."

"You heard what Sally and Phoebe said. Kelly writes in it all the time. We're all in there somewhere. I'm just saying if you *really* wanted to find out what she thinks about you..."

"Razz, it's Kelly's *personal* diary – her private thoughts. There's no way I would read that. No way. It... it wouldn't be right. It'd be... *wrong*. Tell me you're not seriously suggesting I read her diary."

Razza reacted as if he'd been accused of war crimes. "No!" he said, looking wildly around the room. "No, of course not! What do you think I am? No way am I suggesting that you read Kelly's diary... No, no way... Just a leeeeeeeetle bit of it, that's all," he said, holding up his thumb and index finger and moving them together so that they almost touched.

"What!"

"Dude, chill out, okay? It wouldn't be like you were *reading* the diary. You'd be just... gathering necessary *information*. See... it'd be more like... like... *research*. That's it, research – the same thing you do for the debating team all the time. Yeah, just imagine the topic is *That Kelly Faulkner has the hots for Ishmael Leseur* and you need to get some supporting evidence, that's all."

"I don't believe it. I just don't believe it. This is unbelievable, even for you. You're actually calling poking around in Kelly's most private thoughts *research*?"

"Sure... and anyway, you'll be doing her a favour."

"Doing her a favour!"

"Yeah. Look, if you read the diary and find out she's hot for you, then you can go for it and you'll both be happy, right? Then again, if you read the diary and find out that the sight of you makes her want to chuck up, then you can stop harassing her and she'll still be happy *plus* you won't make a complete idiot of yourself. See what I'm getting at, man? It's a win, win, win, win situation."

"Razz, it doesn't matter how you explain it, you're asking me to read Kelly's personal diary and I'm not going to do it."

"I'm not *asking* you to do anything, dude. I'm just pointing out to you a window of opportunity, that's all."

Razza picked up his rucksack and leaned in close to me. "Look, she'd never know, man, so what's the harm? Tell you what I'll do. I'll hang around right outside the door. I can see the stairs from there. Soon as I see feet coming down, I'll thump on the door and give you *plenty* of warning. No sweat. You can't get caught. It'll just take a couple of seconds and then you'll know exactly what Kelly thinks about you. That's what you want, isn't it? Well, here's your window of opportunity, man. Here's your chance to climb right through. Up to you, of course… but I know what I'd do."

He stepped outside, then stuck his head back through the narrow opening of the door. "I'll be right here," he said with a wink then added, "She'll never know, dude."

When the door clicked shut I was alone – alone, that is, except for a small red book that could tell me the one thing I desperately wanted to know.

34.
A Bottom-dwelling Scum-sucker

No way! I told myself. No way was I going to read Kelly Faulkner's diary.

I sniffed at the thought of it, pushed my jumper into my rucksack and hoisted it over one shoulder. The diary was there on the desk in front of me. I reached out and felt the soft velvety suede with my fingers. I glanced over at the closed door. No way!

If Razza thought I would read Kelly's diary, he was dreaming. See, I could even pick it up and hold it in both hands and not be tempted to flip it open and start poking around inside… even though what I wanted to know so badly was just a few easily flicked pages away.

I turned it over a couple of times. I tugged gently at the thin red ribbon that marked the last entry. The diary edged open. I saw some words. No way!

I pulled the ribbon a little harder. The diary sort of opened itself… just like it *wanted* to be read. I saw some cute drawings… poems… and words… lots of words. But I didn't read any of them. No way!

I slammed it shut. I shot another look over at the closed door. The cover felt smooth and soft in my hands. I opened it up again and flipped back a few pages towards the date when we met at Sally's place. I wasn't reading. I was researching. Researching about love. Yes, that's right. I was a serious researcher in the web of love. Either that or a bottom-dwelling scum-sucker. Who, me? No way!

That was it. No more. I'd decided to close the diary for good when one last page fell over – and I saw 'Razza' in capital letters followed by some writing. The words 'crazy' and 'hilarious' caught my eye and something about Sally. No, what was I doing? This was wrong, wrong, wrong! I made up my mind to stop, to walk away. But then… there it was. My name in capital letters at the bottom of the page. No way…

My heart was climbing up into my throat. My eyes drifted down. I began to read.

ISHMAEL

*I always thought Ishmael was a nice guy especially after what he did for Marty – though I must admit, some pretty **weird** things seem to happen to him – eg Sally's pool! But now that I've got to know him a bit better, I think that he's…*

This was key information for my research – crucial. I was about to turn the page to read the rest of the entry when I heard the door squeak open.

"Ishmael, your…"

Kelly Faulkner's smile collapsed as her eyes dropped down to her diary. I slapped it closed. It tumbled from my hands. I snatched at it and caught it with the second grab. I stood there with it clutched in my hands. Some of the pages had been creased and buckled.

"… mother's… here…"

I stood deathly still. There was no other option. I was dead anyway. I watched as Kelly's face knotted in confusion. She looked at me like a little girl who'd just been robbed by the Tooth Fairy.

"You're reading my diary?" It wasn't really a question. More a statement of utter disbelief.

"No... I... It's not like that... I... I just... I... I..."

"You're reading my diary," Kelly stated again, this time as bluntly as a prosecuting attorney.

"Well yes, but... I'm not... It's not... what you think... I... I... I..."

Kelly cut through me with her ice-blue eyes and they were cold and hard and sharp. "You're reading my diary," she said finally, as if all her emotions had been drained from her.

"Kelly... I... I didn't read much... really... hardly anything... I..."

She walked over slowly and took it from me. She kept her head bowed as she opened it, carefully unfolded the creased and crumpled pages and closed it up again.

"Kelly... I'm sorry... I... I..."

And that's when my evil fairy godmother granted my wish because Kelly Faulkner raised her head, looked deep into my eyes and spoke my name with real passion.

"Piss off, Ishmael," she said, and left.

35.
Bummer!

"**M**an, I just cannot believe you read her diary!" I'm telling you now, that if it hadn't been for the fact that it was Mr Barker sitting behind the teacher's desk and we were supposed to be working quietly, it's highly likely that Razza would, at that moment, have been extracting my Social Studies textbook from deep within a cavity of his body not normally associated with reading.

"What!" I whispered back between clenched teeth as I ducked down behind the ample cover provided by Bill Kingsley. "The whole thing was *your* idea, remember. Just read a *little* bit, you said. It's only *research*, you said. I'd be doing her a favour, you said. It's what you'd do, you said."

"Yeah, well, that's right, *I'd* do it, sure. I just didn't believe that *you'd* do it. Man, sprung reading Kelly's private stuff – bummer!"

There was a scrape and shuffle of sound from the teacher's desk and we both buried our eyes in our textbooks and did a furious pantomime of note-taking. I knew I'd regret telling Razza what happened on the weekend, but he'd been pestering me all morning to explain why Kelly had acted so strangely as we were leaving. I'd finally cracked just before Mr Barker marched in for the first lesson.

When it seemed safe to continue I crouched down a little and turned to Razza. "Hey Razz, by the way, can you run through that win, win, win, win situation just one more time for me? I think I may have missed something. Like the bit where I become the world's biggest loser."

"Well, don't blame yourself – it was just bad luck."

"Blame myself? Blame myself? I'm blaming *you*! What happened to *I'll be right outside the door? I'll give you plenty of warning? Don't worry, you won't get caught?*"

"Yeah, well, I had to take a leak, didn't I? And anyway, who would've thought *you* of all people would read some chick's private diary?" Razza clicked his tongue. "Geez, I gotta be honest with you, man. As far as you and the Kelster go, this is a mega setback."

I glared at the bobbing head beside me. "Setback!" I hissed. (Yes, I really did hiss.) "Setback! The *Titanic* and the iceberg – *that* was a setback. The Alamo – that was a setback. Custer at Little Bighorn – they were *all* setbacks. Me getting caught with my nose stuck in Kelly's diary – that's a disaster! Oh, and just in case you were wondering, there were no survivors."

A slight screeching noise came from the front of the room. Mr Barker had pushed his chair back from the desk and was looking in our direction. Razza immediately became intensely interested in his textbook while his finger tracked swiftly along the lines of words. Then he frowned and stroked his chin and gazed off into the distance as if he were contemplating the greatest mysteries of the universe. Finally his face lit up like a light bulb and he jabbed his index finger into the air to signal some burst of inspiration. This was followed by a flurry of scribbling in his notebook. All in all it was the worst display of overacting since Roger Rabbit tried out for the lead role in *Hamlet*.

It seemed to do the trick, though. Mr Barker shifted his chair forward and returned to the papers he was marking. I decided to try to block the diary disaster from my mind by burying myself in the thrilling and fascinating world of the federal parliamentary system. My efforts were interrupted by a nudge on my arm.

"Hey Ishmael, I just remembered. I brought this back for you."

Razza dug down deep into his shorts pocket and pulled something out. He sneaked a look at Mr Barker then handed it over. It was the Dugongs cassette he'd borrowed.

"Man, you know these guys are pretty cool. Not *exactly* my thing, but they're tight all right and some of their stuff really rocks. Anyway, I hope your dad doesn't mind, but I made my own copy. I've been using it to…"

"Mister Zorzotto!"

The entire room cringed. Mr Barker's voice had that effect.

"Would you mind coming out the front and bringing whatever it is that you and Mr Leseur are so taken by?"

My heart tore away from my chest cavity and did a base dive to the pit of my stomach. Every eye in the classroom followed Razza as he moved down the aisle and placed the cassette on the desk in front of Mr Barker.

"Sit down, Mr Zorzotto."

As Razza slid in beside me I watched Mr Barker pick up the tape and slowly turn it over in his hand. He looked our way. "Mr Zorzotto and Mr Leseur – you will *both* be remaining behind when the class is dismissed."

Razza continued to pretend to read his textbook as he whispered out of the side of his mouth. "Now *that's* a disaster."

And for the first time that morning, the Razzman and I were of one mind.

36.
The Towering
Inferno

Razza and I kept working as the rest of the class filtered out of the room.

Then Mr Barker called us over to his desk. "Mr Zorzotto, Mr Leseur, I trust that the sound of all your classmates working quietly and diligently during that lesson didn't spoil your conversation too much?"

"No Sir, no worries," Razza said without thinking. "Well… not that we were really having a conversation or anything like that. I was just asking Ishmael about… you know… the stuff we were reading about."

"And exactly which 'stuff' might that have been, Mr Zorzotto?"

"Well, Sir, mainly… you know all that stuff about… the government… and how there's local, state and feral government… and how they… govern… and stuff…"

'Thank you, Mr Zorzotto,' Mr Barker said with a thin smile. 'For a moment there I was worried that my teaching wasn't making a real difference to the world, but just being in the presence of such a knowledgeable, articulate young man like yourself, I can see I was mistaken."

"Gee thanks, Sir. I've learned loads of stuff in your lessons."

"Don't mention it… to anyone… please."

Then Mr Barker held up the cassette. "Now, explain this to me, Mr Zorzotto, and how it came to be in your possession."

"Well sir, I wasn't doing anything really. I was just giving it back to Ishmael, because he lent it to me on account of his dad's in the band and I…"

Mr Barker's head swung my way. "Your *father* was in the band?"

The intense glare of Mr Barker's eyes made me want to deny that I even had a father, but before I could come up with an answer he'd levelled his index finger at me. "Leseur… yes, yes of course… Leseur. I don't believe it.

You mean to say that your father is… the Towering Inferno?"

Razza and I exchanged a look. It was obvious to both of us that the pressure of being Deputy Principal at St Daniel's had taken its toll and that poor Mr Barker had finally gone barking mad. I was just hoping that things didn't turn really nasty before the guys in the white jackets showed up. I smiled nervously at the pair of crazy eyes before me.

"The Towering Inferno," Mr Barker said again as if that would help. "That's what they called him because of the red hair… and because he was so tall."

Razza and I looked at each other and then back at Mr Barker.

"Your father… Ronnie 'The Red' Leseur… lead singer of The Dugongs."

"You *know* them Sir?" Razza asked.

"*Know* them? Of course I know them. During my university days The Dugongs were huge. I've got a vinyl copy of this album at home – more scratches than grooves now."

Mr Barker stared at the cassette case and seemed to drift away in his own thoughts. "We used to travel miles to see the 'Gongs. They were fantastic... "Dead Toad Society Blues", 'Bad Day for Angels', 'Collision Course'... Great days... magic days..."

Mr Barker stopped and looked up at Razza, whose mouth hung open like the loading door of a cargo plane. "Yes, Mr Zorzotto, as impossible as it may be for you to comprehend, there once was a time in my life when I used to be a human being."

"*Really* Sir?" Razza said with perhaps a tad too much amazement.

"Yes, really," Mr Barker growled, morphing for a moment into his old self.

"No, Sir... what I meant was... that it's *really* good... 'cause I think they're pretty cool too. That's exactly what I was telling Ishmael when you... You know, when you... Anyway... I think it's wicked that they're getting back together again."

"The Dugongs are reuniting?" Mr Barker fired the question at me.

"Yes, Sir."

"When? Where?"

I hadn't seen Mr Barker this excited since the day he put an entire busload of boys on afternoon detention for unruly behaviour.

"In about a month... somewhere in town. They're having a big meeting this weekend to sort it all out, tickets and stuff."

"And they've got all the original members?"

"Except the drummer."

"Yes... Yes, of course... a terrible thing..."

Mr Barker was lost in his thoughts for a moment before snapping back to life. "Mr Leseur, you must promise to do something for me under pain of death."

I agreed. It was no big deal. I just naturally assumed that everything you did for Mr Barker was under pain of death.

"You must keep me informed about the reunion. I want to know the minute tickets become available. Do you understand?"

"No problem, Sir."

Razza and I just stood there for a while as Mr Barker twirled the cassette case in his hands, every now and then either nodding or shaking his head.

"Um... can we... go now, Sir?"

"Oh... right... yes... Yes, Mr Zorzotto... Yes, you may both go."

Then Mr Barker seemed to climb back into his old skin before our eyes. "But be warned, I shall be checking your notebooks thoroughly tomorrow, so make sure everything is up to date. And in future if you waste your time chatting during my lessons when you should be working, you can expect a lunchtime detention. Is that clear?"

"Yes, Sir," we said together.

"And of course I will have to confiscate this. You may pick it up at the front office at the end of the week, Mr Leseur. Good morning, gentlemen."

We left Mr Barker huddled over his desk still gazing at the old cassette.

Outside, Razza looked at me in amazement. "Are you on drugs?"

"No."

"Me either. So unless we're both having exactly the same dream, it means that what happened in there really did happen."

I knew what Razza was getting at. It was like I said. You just couldn't trust people any more to behave the way they were supposed to. The list was growing. I could add Mr Barker to Barry Bagsley, my father, and Scobie.

It was as if I had entered another dimension and was living in the Twilight Zone.

"Mr Barker's a Dugongs fan," I said, shaking my head.

"Yeah," Razza said, shaking his even more, "and a human being."

37.
As Popular as a Rotting Corpse

It took a lot of work, but Razza finally persuaded me to go along with him to support Lourdes College in their semi-final debate as we promised we would. When he also suggested that I might like to bring his poem along as a "secret weapon", I took great pleasure in informing him that my treasured copy of 'Hot or what!' had somehow tragically and mysteriously vanished and that I wouldn't be volunteering to lead the search party to look for it.

By the time Mrs Zorzotto dropped us off and we found the right room, both teams were already in position nervously murmuring away or doing last-minute checks of their index cards, so we grabbed a couple of spare seats towards the back of the packed room. When Sally saw us, she gave Razza a big smile and a wave. Then she touched Kelly's hand and whispered something to her. Kelly looked our way and gave a half-smile then returned to her notes. A cold front moved through the room and a large depression settled right on top of me.

I can't even remember what the topic was that night, and the debate itself was a blur. All I remember is watching every move Kelly made and every emotion that played out on her face. She was only the length of a room away, but every time I thought of her last words to me, she might as well have been on the other side of the universe.

This much I do remember about the debate, though – the girls lost.

When it was all over we hung back a little until the huddle of family and friends began to thin out, then Razza dragged me forward to where Sally and Kelly were talking with their parents. Mr and Mrs Nofke and Mr and Mrs Faulkner said hello to us before telling the girls not to be too long and drifting off downstairs.

That left just the four of us in the classroom, but it felt nothing like that afternoon under the pergola at Kelly's house when everything was so easy. Now Razza and Sally had to struggle to fill up the embarrassing silences while Kelly stood there looking uncomfortable and I felt about as popular as a rotting corpse. Razza really did his best to lighten the mood, but it was a bit like being Tickle-me Elmo at a funeral.

"You guys were great. Man, those judges didn't know what they were talking about. I think they just ran out of fingers when they were trying to add up your score. Just wait till next year, hey Kelly?"

Kelly squeezed out a smile that vanished almost the instant it appeared.

"Yeah, that's right, man. Just you wait, you'll see – there'll be no stopping you guys. What d'ya reckon, Ishmael?"

"That's right."

"Yeah – no stopping you. The other teams probably won't even bother showing up." Razza looked desperately around the three of us searching for a spark of life.

Sally came to his rescue. "Well, look on the bright side, at least we've got our lives back now and we won't have to spend all our lunchtimes and weekends working on debating, hey Kel?"

Kelly cranked out another manufactured smile.

"That's right, man. I reckon you guys *paid* the adjudicators to give the debate to the other team just so you could chill out and party."

Sally laughed. Kelly didn't.

"Hey, that reminds me," Sally said. "Kel, isn't there a school dance on this Friday?"

"I think you may be right," Kelly said with a strange expression on her face.

"Yes, I think I am… This Friday… and I'm fairly sure it's the last one for the year, isn't it?"

"It certainly is," Kelly said, as if she was repeating lines from a play.

"Well, now that we don't have to worry about preparing for the final or anything, maybe we should go along. What do you say?"

"Maybe," Kelly said without enthusiasm. "I'll see what Brad says."

The sound of Brad's name went through me like a cruise missile.

"Right… I guess I'll probably have to go by myself,"

Sally said, then shot a quick look at Razza, who was bobbing around waiting for an opportunity to jump back into the conversation with a one-liner.

"Yes, I suppose I'll just have to tag along with you and Brad... Unless, of course, I can *bribe* someone to go with me."

Razza's eyes lit up. "*Bribe* someone to go with you?"

Sally smiled shyly at him.

"Where would you get that kind of money from? What, did you win first prize in the lottery or something?" Razza laughed and then grinned at each of us in turn.

Nobody grinned back.

I wasn't grinning because I'd seen the dark cloud that had engulfed Kelly's face. And Kelly wasn't grinning because she'd seen the red blush seeping into Sally's cheeks and the sparkle switching off in her eyes.

Sally managed a lopsided smile. "Yes... I guess that's right, isn't it? Just like you said... I'd need loads of money, wouldn't I? I mean, who in their right mind would want to go to the dance... with me..."

Those last two words sort of crumbled from Sally's mouth and awful silent tears began to pool in her eyes.

Kelly reached forward. "Sal, don't…" But she was already turning and rushing from the room.

Kelly spun round and glared at Razza. "You want some advice, Orazio?" she said as if she'd been taking voice coaching with Mr Barker. "You know that enormous *chasm* between your ears? Well maybe you should advertise it for rent. You know, something like: huge, empty space – some sawdust to be removed – *never been used*."

Razza spread his arms wide. "But… But what did I do?"

"What did you *do*? Has it ever occurred to you that Sally actually *likes* you?"

"But I… I like *her*."

"*Really, really* likes you?"

Razza's eyes began drifting around as if they were trying to latch on to something that made sense to them. "But I really… I just… I didn't think…"

"Tell me about it," Kelly said coldly. "You didn't catch on at the party? Or when we asked you over to help out with the debating? Or just now when Sally practically *begged* you to take her to the dance? Hello! Earth to Orazio! Do you read me?"

Kelly shook her head and made for the door. She was about to push it open when she stopped and turned a pair of tired, pale eyes on both of us. "Didn't you guys used to be superheroes or something?"

The door swung open then eased closed and Kelly was gone. I looked back at Razza and waited for those crazy lights to burn in his eyes once again or for the killer smile to ignite or the smart comeback to be fired off. But there was none of that. Instead he just slumped down on the chair beside him like a rag doll and looked up at me with a face like a busted balloon.

"She *really* liked me," he mumbled as if they were his dying words.

Orazio Zorzotto had just been trampled by an elephant of surprise.

38.
It Comes!

"Ishmael, for god's sake... do something!"

It was Ignatius Prindabel. He'd cornered me out in the playground and now he was hovering around like a mad wasp while I tried to eat my lunch. I was sitting on a bench near the gym as he paced back and forth in front of me, raking his long fingers through his stringy hair.

It was all because of Razza.

"It's got to stop. It must. Even when he was 'normal' he was unbearable, but this... this is *torture*!"

Ignatius was right, of course. It was over a week since the night of the debating semi-final, and Razza was still walking around like a death-row prisoner who'd just been told his final meal would be stewed broccoli.

"But what can I do?"

"Anything... something!"

Right, let's see. Oh, I know, perhaps I could use my fine standing in the community to write a reference for him.

> *Dear Sally*
> *I have known Orazio Zorzotto for over two years now, and as a suspected pool piddler and convicted diary perver, I feel well qualified to speak on behalf of his good character...*

Yep, that'd help loads.

Prindabel shoved his hands into his pockets and scrunched up his shoulders. "I don't understand. You told us that this girl actually likes him, right?"

"Right."

"Well then, why doesn't he just apologise? He could even send her one of those *rigid* poems to make up. I mean, *we* all know they're crap, but she'll probably think he's a genius. After all, if she likes Orazio then she's hardly going to be a member of Mensa, is she?"

"Sally gets straight A's and tops her class *and* she got an Outstanding Achievement Certificate in the National Maths Competition last year."

Prindabel looked at me as if I'd just informed him that Einstein was a cross-dresser. "But you said she likes Orazio?"

"That's right."

"But she's… *intelligent*."

"Yep."

"But she likes *Orazio*."

"That's right."

"But…"

We seemed to be caught in a loop.

"Look, Ignatius, I think that's the problem. Razza just doesn't know what to do because he doesn't think he's smart enough for her."

"Well that goes without saying, but it doesn't help us, does it? Look, you're his friend. *You* have to talk to him – you can't let him mope around like this for the rest of his life. It's excruciating… It's nauseating… It's… It's…"

Suddenly Ignatius lifted his head and looked past

me into the distance. Then he raised his arm slowly and pointed with a trembling finger. "It comes!" he croaked.

I twisted round and saw Razza on the other side of the playground drifting his way towards us. When I turned back the bent form of Ignatius Prindabel was loping away in the opposite direction, casting hurried glances back over his shoulder like an extra from a Godzilla movie.

Moments later Razza flopped down on the bench beside me and sat there without speaking.

"How's it going, Razz?"

He shrugged his shoulders.

"You okay?"

Another shoulder shrug.

"Look, you're not still beating yourself up about Sally and the other night, are you?"

Those shoulders were certainly getting a workout.

"Razz, come on, why don't you just ring her up, say you're sorry and explain to her that it was all just a stupid joke?"

"Some joke, man."

"She'll understand. You heard what Kelly said – she really likes you."

"*Liked* me, you mean. You think anyone with a brain like hers would seriously want to hang around with someone so stupid he doesn't realise when he's being asked out?"

I looked at the lifeless form slumped beside me. The Twilight Zone had claimed another victim. "Come on. This is stupid," I said. "This isn't like you. What happened to the Razzman? The Big Z? The social worker for love? The child of the universe?"

There was quite a wait before Razza replied, but when he did I knew that it wasn't the Razzman or the Big Z or any of those other guys who was speaking to me.

"I made her cry, man."

"Yeah… I know, Razz, but you didn't mean…"

"My old man used to make my mum cry all the time – before he pissed off for good. He was always yelling… and doing other stuff… and then he'd go off and we wouldn't see him for days. I hated it when Mum cried… so I'd tell her jokes and muck around and make stupid faces, anything to get a laugh out of her. That was my job – making my mum laugh. I got pretty good at it too. But then the old man'd come back and ruin everything and Mum would start crying all over again. Man, I swore I'd never be like him." Razza flicked a bit of twig away. "He finally got lost when I was eight. Left us nothing but his old drum kit… he was good at beating things. And you know what, man? I was glad. I was glad he was gone."

Just then the end-of-lunch bell came blaring across the playground.

Razza pulled himself to his feet and looked down at me with a face as cold as a tombstone. "I made her cry, man," he said. "How's that thing go… like father, like son?"

Track 8:
The Time
has Come

The time has come
To stand up and be counted
The time has come
To burn our wings upon the sun
The time has come
The bugle charge has sounded
It's all been said and done
Now the time has come

From The Dugongs: *Returned & Remastered*
Music & lyrics: W. Mangan and R. Leseur

39.
The Crown Prince
of 'Go-to' Men

Prindabel was right. I had to do something about Razza. I'd never seen anyone so down. Well, at least I hadn't until two nights later at home when I came face to face with The Dugongs.

Apparently the big meeting that I'd told Mr Barker about hadn't gone too well. Even though their old manager promised them that everything was under control, there was still no sign of tickets, and the advertising brochures hadn't arrived from the printer. Dad's worries were galloping into panic. With about a month to go before the big night he called an emergency meeting at our place to make sure all the arrangements were definitely in place. That's what I walked in on.

I looked around the room. Uncle Ray was on the couch – a bit beefier and balder than he used to be – sort of a feral Santa Claus. Slumped down beside him with his long thin legs stretching halfway across the room was Leo McCrae. Judging by his hair and clothes, it was a pretty safe bet that Leo's favourite colour was black. Sitting opposite them alongside my father was the new drummer Mick Stallybrass – not much taller than me but with biceps as big as his shaved head.

"Dad, Mum wants to know if anyone wants a tea or coffee." Then I remembered Mr Barker. "Oh, and are the tickets on sale yet, because the Deputy Principal at school keeps asking me about them and…"

"I think you can forget about the concert."

Four gloomy faces avoided eye contact. Dad was out-glooming all the rest. I waited to see if it was some kind of a joke. Nobody laughed.

"What do you mean?"

Dad shook his head as if it was too much effort to explain, so Uncle Ray took over. "Well, it seems Alex, our esteemed manager, has decided to bugger off with all the money we gave him and leave us up a certain creek without a paddle."

"He stole your money?"

"Yessireeeee bob," Uncle Ray said with a cheesy grin.

"Why would he do that?"

"You know, I'm not sure," Uncle Ray said, "but I've got a feeling that maybe he's just not a nice man."

Mick nodded. "Well, he was always dirty on you guys for splitting up, wasn't he – always whingeing about missing out on the big bucks. I guess he thought he'd hop in for his chop early this time and avoid the rush."

"Bastard," Leo drawled – apparently a man of few words as well as few colours.

"But can't you have the concert anyway?"

Uncle Ray sucked his teeth. "Well, that might be a *little* difficult. It appears that as well as being a thief, our manager is also a scabby lying dog. It seems that he didn't book the venue like he said or place ads in any local papers or arrange to have posters made up or make contact with any media outlets. To give him his due though, he did manage to sell a couple of hundred fake tickets in the last few days and pocket the profits. And of course, let's not forget the master stroke –

all our amps have mysteriously disappeared." Uncle Ray pushed his fingers down the sides of his bushy moustache and frowned. "You think maybe it's just a coincidence?"

I looked at my father. For the second time in a couple of days I found myself facing a pair of defeated eyes. I kept thinking about what Mum had said, about Dad wanting and needing this reunion, even though it frightened him, and I had the terrible feeling that if it didn't happen now it might never happen. I didn't need Prindabel shouting at me to do something. I was shouting it at myself.

"Well... why don't you... book another place... and just hire the stuff you need... Go ahead anyway?"

"We've been through all that, mate," Dad said, rubbing his forehead. "To get a hall that holds even a few hundred people, with all the right sound and lighting gear, you have to book months in advance. There's just none available – believe me, we tried. And even if we had a venue, we're still in the middle of rehearsing. There's just not enough time for us to organise all the publicity and ticketing and everything else. Not to mention the fact that we're already thousands of dollars out of pocket. And we can't leave it any later, otherwise it's too close to Christmas. So that takes care of this year. And if we don't do it this year it wouldn't really be a twenty-year reunion concert, so what'd be the point?"

"I hate to say it, little buddy, but I think your dad may be right," Uncle Ray said. "A bit under four weeks – it's nowhere near enough time to start from scratch. So unless you happen to know of some organisational genius who just might be willing to work their butt off for nothing to help get a concert up and running on the smell of an oily rag – oh, preferably someone with their very own concert hall would be nice – then I'm afraid, as they say in show biz, we are well and truly stuffed."

"Buggered," Leo added.

But I wasn't really listening, because a strange thought had begun to struggle to life in my head. "So... What you really need... is sort of like... a 'go-to' man?" I asked.

"Well," Uncle Ray said, puffing out a breath, "I'd say more like the crown prince of 'go-to' men."

"Right... And would it help a bit... if he was also a big Dugongs fan?"

Uncle Ray eyed me suspiciously. "Don't suppose it would hurt."

My strange thought looked like it might survive. It was a bit wobbly but it seemed to be standing up. I was thinking that when I noticed everyone looking at me as if I had two heads. It was probably because I was the only one in the room who was smiling.

"I know just the guy," I told them.

40.
Leave it with Me
(Twice)

On Monday morning before school I went to see Mr Barker in his office. In the end I didn't even have to ask him if he would help with the concert. As soon as I'd finished explaining what had happened to The Dugongs his eyes started to dart about and then they stopped and zeroed in on me. "They can have it here," he said. "In the gym. Need to run it by Brother Jerome, of course... and three to four weeks could be tricky... but not impossible... Leave it with me."

That night Mr Barker rang to say that Brother Jerome had given his approval and that not only was the gym available, but because the end-of-year assembly/mass/prize-giving/speech night/extravaganza thingy would be held there a few days later, most of the stage, lighting and sound would already be in place.

But my father still wasn't convinced. "He's a deputy principal, for crying out loud – a teacher – not a band manager or a concert promoter. He's way out of his depth."

Dad finally agreed under protest when Mum pointed out that when it came to managing The Dugongs, Mr Barker didn't have a whole lot to live up to.

Just two nights later we were all in the lounge room – Dad and the rest of The Dugongs, Mum, Prue and me – watching Mr Barker pull a typed sheet of paper from his briefcase and lay it on the coffee table in front of him. It was a progress report on the arrangements for the concert.

"Right, as I said, the gym's available and most of the staging, lighting and sound will be set up. We've got plenty of volunteers from staff and students to help operate everything – and they're used to handling musical productions and rock festivals, so that's all under control."

"What's it costing us to rent the hall?" Uncle Ray asked.

"Nothing."

"Nothing? How'd you swing that with the boss?"

"I convinced him we wouldn't be out of pocket – in fact we stand to generate a reasonable profit. We're making parking available on the lower oval for a small fee – Mr Guthrie and some of the boarders will be organising that. No alcohol will be allowed inside the gym but the Parents and Friends have a licence to operate a bar on the tennis courts. In addition to the bar, they will be manning a food and drinks stall outside in the playground. They also intend to run raffles throughout the night and sell a range of college memorabilia. Zoe Tarango is coordinating all that for me. As for the overall ticket sales, I propose that ten per cent of the total earnings go to the college to help cover any additional costs."

Dad looked around at the other band members, who nodded in stunned silence.

"Look, that sounds... great," Dad said, "but are you sure you know what you're taking on here? A rock concert can be a bit... wild. It's a big ask."

Mr Barker looked steadily at my father. "You haven't had the pleasure of attending one of our gym dances, have you? Six hundred hormone-ravaged teenagers let loose in semi-darkness. Perhaps I could put you down as a volunteer parent supervisor and you could experience it for yourself."

Dad was quiet for a moment then he tapped the sheet of paper on the coffee table. "What's the next item on the agenda?"

"Let's see," Mr Barker said, ticking off a few points, "Publicity. Now as far as that goes, I've taken the liberty of putting together a feature article about the band and the reunion concert for the college newsletter. It goes out tomorrow to over 1200 families, so that's a start. I've included a leaflet as well for people to display in shops, workplaces etc etc. Now I've also provided a copy of the article to the St Daniel's Old Boys Association, and they are contacting all their members in the print media and radio, so we should get a fair bit of free coverage there. Not sure about television, but I'm working on that. Obviously I've emphasised the change of venue and made it clear we would honour any tickets that have been sold previously or refund money if necessary."

Mr Barker stabbed another tick on the sheet.

"Right, the next thing is that Carla Lagilla from the

Art department is keen to get her students involved, so they'll be creating posters and a backdrop for the stage area. She also wanted to know if you would be agreeable to her designing and printing a special commemorative T-shirt that could be sold on the night to help raise funds for a big Art excursion that's arranged for next year."

Dad glanced around again. Everyone was staring at Mr Barker as if he'd just parted the Red Sea.

"No… No problem… That'd be fine… Great."

Another tick.

"Now then, naturally Mr Carlson and the Music department are right behind us. They've arranged for a private rehearsal room to be made available for the band at the college any time over the next three weeks as well as equipment if you need it. There was also a suggestion that if you had time, a few music students might be able to sit in on some practices, and perhaps you could speak to a couple of the classes – but that's entirely up to you. On the night itself Mr Carlson has lined up the school big band as well as two of our best student rock groups as support acts. We thought they could play from seven till around eight, then you would go from eight-thirty. How does all that sound?"

Dad spoke for all the stunned faces and shaking heads in the room. "Amazing."

"Good, well that about covers everything I wanted to say at this stage. There's still a lot to be done, details to iron out, but I think I can say that we're on target." As Mr Barker began to gather up his stuff the stunned faces softened into smiles.

"Look, Mr Barker... Phil..." Dad said, "you've done so much already. It's unbelievable. We sure could have used you twenty years ago. How can we ever make it up to you?"

Mr Barker looked up. "Just do two things... and that will be more than enough," he said. "Play the concert... " and then he reached into his briefcase and pulled out an old vinyl album with a fading photograph of The Dugongs on the front cover, "and do me the honour of signing this."

When all the Dugongs had written their names and messages on the album cover, Mr Barker clipped his briefcase shut and said his goodbyes. But as he was about to leave, he hesitated. "You know, there is one other thing you could do for me if you wouldn't mind."

"Name it," Dad said.

"Well, it might sound silly... but it's just... When I'm speaking to people about the band and the concert, it can get a bit confusing when I say I'm the Deputy Principal of St Daniel's... so I was wondering if you'd mind at all... if just for the time being, just until after the concert... I might officially refer to myself as... the manager of The Dugongs?"

Dad didn't need to check with the others this time. "We wouldn't want it any other way," he said.

Mr Barker bobbed his head in a way that for a disturbing second reminded me of Razza, and then something extraordinary happened to his face. It let itself smile.

If Dad or any of the other Dugongs had any lingering doubts about Mr Barker, then they were all swiftly knocked on the head over the next couple of weeks. As well as advertising posters for the reunion appearing everywhere, the local radio station began plugging the concert and a popular afternoon TV programme did a special feature on the band. With less than one week to go before the big night, over a thousand tickets had been sold – more than double what the group had ever dared to hope for.

But Mr Barker wasn't the only one who was getting things organised. I had finally decided to take Prindabel's advice and "do something" about Razza. That was why after school one day I handed Ignatius a large envelope with Sally Nofke's name printed on the front. Inside it were three things: a leaflet advertising The Dugongs' reunion, a double pass to the concert and a note from Razza that simply said 'I'm sorry'.

After I explained all that to Ignatius he held the envelope in his hand and frowned. "Do you really think this will work?"

"Not sure. All I know is that Razza will be there – so will Bill and Scobie – but whether Sally turns up... who knows?"

"Maybe he should have written something more than just 'I'm sorry'?"

"Maybe, but it was hard enough getting him to do that much. He reckoned it was just going to end up in the bin anyway. Look, Ignatius, just get your sister to take it to school and pass it on to Sally Nofke, okay, and we'll hope for the best."

"Right... sure," Ignatius said vaguely as he continued to frown down at the envelope. "Leave it with me."

So that's what I did.

But there was something else that I left with Ignatius that day. Tucked inside Sally's envelope was a smaller one with Kelly Faulkner's name on it and inside that was another leaflet advertising the reunion, another double pass to the concert and another note – from me this time – that simply said 'I'm sorry'.

You see, my father wasn't the only one who had everything riding on the return of The Dugongs.

41.
One Plus One

The night of The Dugongs' reunion concert was cloudy and humid. Razza and I had spent most of the day helping Mr Barker get things set up before sitting in on the band's final run-through. They sounded good too, but I was still worried by the look of quiet panic in Dad's eyes.

When we returned that evening about a half an hour before the first of the school groups kicked off, a large crowd was already spilling into the playground and more were filing up from the bottom oval car park. While Mum and Prue went with Dad straight to the rehearsal room, Razza and I decided to head to the gym.

We were checking some of Ms Lagilla's posters when a familiar voice came from behind us.

"Leseur... Zorzotto... there you are."

We turned to see a lanky form dressed in a school uniform squinting at us.

"Ignatius, what are you doing here? I didn't think you were into rock music."

"I'm not. I'm one of the volunteers they're forcing to help out in the car park. Just finished my shift. Now I'm on the merchandising stall – thought I'd bring some of the Pi Club T-shirts along to sell."

There was a pause. I think both Ignatius and I expected a comment from Razza at this point – something along the lines of, "You brought Mathematics T-shirts to a rock concert? What's your next marketing venture, Prindabel? Selling Barbie dolls to the Marines?"

But nothing came. Ever since the incident with Sally it was as if someone had pushed Razza's mute button. I was about to say something when a large group of people drifting into the gym distracted me.

"Razza, look."

I pointed towards the back of the hall where Sally Nofke was having her ticket checked. Behind her were her parents and behind them was Kelly Faulkner. My heart bounded from a giant springboard and shot in the air. Then I saw Brad and it bellyflopped straight back into an empty pool.

Sally moved further inside and waited for the others.

"She came…" Razza said as if he was in shock.

Ignatius leaned forward and whispered disturbingly close to my ear, "Is *that* her?"

I nodded.

"But she's… she's…"

"I know."

He turned and had another look.

"*And* she's intelligent."

"Uh-huh."

"And she likes Orazio?"

Here we go again.

Just then Sally looked right at us and gave a quick wave. Then she spoke briefly with Kelly and her parents before threading her way through the crowd in our direction.

Ignatius glanced around nervously. "Ah, Orazio… there's something I should *probably* tell you."

He reached forward and grabbed Razza by the arm.

"Hey, man, what're you…"

"No time to explain – just listen to what I'm saying. *Agree* with her, all right? Whatever she says – just go along with it. You did it, all right. *You* did it. It was all your idea. Got that?"

"Prindabel, what the hell are you…"

But it was too late. Ignatius had scurried off and Sally was zeroing in.

"Well, Razz, I'll leave you to it, okay? Good luck."

A pain stabbed in my bicep. Razza had a death-grip on my arm. "No, Ishmael, wait – I need you, man… Please."

I had no idea what good I could do hanging around, but the look in Razza's eyes told me I wasn't going anywhere.

Sally made her way to us and we exchanged a few awkward greetings. Then she turned to Razza. "Thanks for sending the tickets… and especially for… you know… the other thing." She smiled coyly and looked at the floor.

"The *other* thing," Razza said, leaning in a little. "Right, yeah… the other thing… And that would be the… um… the…"

Sally looped her long dark hair behind her ears and

looked quickly at me. I edged away a little and pretended to be absorbed in watching the crowd.

"Stop trying to embarrass me," she said. "You know what I mean… the poem."

"Oh right," Razza said, throwing back his head and nodding confidently, "the *poem*. Yeah, of course… The poem… Right… *That* other thing."

Sally gave a little laugh then her dark eyes fixed on Razza. "It was… so sweet," she said quietly with a slight shake of her head, "… and so clever."

A manic smile tried to smother the utter confusion on Razza's face. "Really?"

Sally looked down and her black hair fell forward across her cheeks. "It was the nicest thing anyone's ever given me… I keep it with me all the time."

Razza's manic smiled eased back a few notches. "So… what… You mean… you've got it here now?"

She blushed and gave a little nod.

"Can I see it?" Razza asked eagerly.

Sally looked up and wrinkled up her cute nose. "What would you want to see it for?"

"Well, I just… You know, I thought… that um… that ah…" Suddenly more pain surged through my arm and I found myself being yanked sideways, "... that maybe Ishmael here would like to read it."

Sally frowned even more.

"Yeah, I know it's a bit... weird... but the thing is I've been telling him all about it... You know, about the poem and everything... but it's not the same unless you actually read it... So I thought if he could just have a quick squiz at it that's all..."

Sally seemed uncertain. "Well, I *guess* so... if it's all right with you."

"Sure. Ishmael and me are mates – we share everything, don't we, Ishmael?"

I couldn't really disagree – Razza had his hand on the back of my neck and was practically nodding my head for me.

Sally reached into the back pocket of her jeans, pulled out a slip of paper and passed it across. I unfolded it and with Razza peering over my shoulder, we read together.

To Sally...
ONE PLUS ONE
You're the balance to my equation
The answer to my sum

You're the X that I've been seeking
My prime number – number one.

You're my complementary angle
The sine of my cos tan
But I'm just a vulgar fraction
Until you have to understand

That I won't be completed
Till you tell me that you care
Then I'll be your circumference
And you, my pr^2.

Now I'm no mathematician,
So please tell me if it's true
That one plus one together
Can equal me and you.

Razza and I stared at the sheet long after we had
finished reading it.

"That's… just great Razz," I said finally as I handed
the poem back to Sally. She smiled and she bit her
bottom lip. I thought only Kelly Faulkner could look

that beautiful. Razza, on the other hand, looked completely miserable. He was also mumbling something.

"Sorry?" Sally asked, still smiling.

"I didn't write it."

Her smile fell away as if it had lost the will to live.

"The poem… It's not mine… I didn't write it. I wish I had… but… I can't lie to you… I suck at Maths… and everything else."

A shimmer began to appear in Sally's eyes just as it had the night of the debating semi-final. I could hear Prindabel's voice screaming in my head, "Do something!"

"Ah… No, look… Razza's just being modest, Sally… What he's really trying to say is that he had some *help* with the poem… with the Maths stuff. A friend of ours, Ignatius… Ignatius Prindabel… You know, Cynthia Prindabel's brother… Well, he's right into Maths and Razz told me just now how he helped out with the terms and everything… But you know, the *main* ideas… the *meaning* of the poem and what it says… Well, that's all Razza's work."

Sally and I both looked at Razza.

I waited but I didn't get any support. "That's right, isn't it Razz?… The *ideas* in the poem… You know, what it's saying and everything... That comes from you, right? I mean, that's not Prindabel talking, is it? That's what *you* think, right?"

Razza looked at me doubtfully. "Well yeah... but..."

"See Sal, it's just like I said, he's being way too modest. He's always like that. He's famous for it here at St Daniel's. Zorzotto the Humble, we call him."

Sally blinked the shimmer from her eyes and smiled. "Well, that's all right – it's definitely the *thought* that counts."

The beginnings of a smile also appeared on Razza's face. "Look, Sally, about the other night... at the debate... I'm sorry... Man, I was like a total doofus."

"That makes two of us... I guess we should get on really well, hey."

They were both wrapped up in a communal grin-a-thon, so I guessed it was time to make a hasty retreat.

"Well look, I'm gonna go down to the rehearsal room to wish Dad good luck."

"Hey, cool, me too. You wanna come along, Sal?"

"No, no. You two go. I better see what's happened to Kelly and Brad. But when you get back... maybe we could have a dance?"

You could have used Razza's face for the entrance to Disneyworld. "Yeah, cool! Awesome!"

Sally smiled for a second then frowned and sucked in air through her teeth. "Only problem is… since I haven't won the lottery or anything… I'm not sure whether or not I can *afford* you."

Razza's smile flopped down like a closing umbrella.

"I know," Sally said with her face lighting up. "Perhaps I could do a trade with you – you dance with me and I'll give you free Maths tutoring. How does that sound?"

"Rigid!" Razza said, once again in Disneyworld mode. "And you won't regret it either, Sal. You'll see – I'm a wicked dancer. Man, I'm Lord of the Dance!" And to prove his point Razza began to thrash and jerk about like a plague of angry ferrets had invaded his boxer shorts.

Sally turned to me with her eyebrows raised. "Zorzotto the Humble?"

"Yes, well… That was just a *temporary* cover," I said. It was too. The Razzman was back.

42.
Tired of Safe

We left Sally in the gym and headed off to the rehearsal room. By the time we reached the door Razza was his old self. It seemed as good a time as any to bring up something that had been bothering me.

"Hey, Razza... you know that stuff you said about your dad... and your mum and everything?"

He threw a cautious look my way. "Yeah..."

"Well... you know that bit about your dad making your mum cry?"

"Yeah..."

"I was just wondering... Do you think he ever felt as bad as you did... you know... about Sally?"

Razza gave me a sad kind of smile. "Him? I doubt it. If he did, he wouldn't have kept doing it, would he?"

"Yeah… yeah, that's what I thought."

Razza rested his hand on the door handle as he studied my face.

"What are you getting at, Ishmael?"

"It's just, that thing you said, 'like father, like son'? Well… I don't reckon you're anything like your father at all. I really don't."

Razza smiled. "Thanks, man. But you know, I gotta admit, I did get some good things from my dad."

"Like what?"

"Well, obviously, my drop-dead-gorgeous, movie-star, heart-throb, teen-mag hunk good looks for one."

"Yes, well, *that* goes without saying."

Razza pushed down on the handle and opened the door. "*And* I inherited his one and only talent."

I was almost afraid to ask what that might be, but as it turned out, I didn't get the chance. As the door swung open we found ourselves right in the heart of Worry Central.

Prue and Mum were sitting huddled together on a desk, Uncle Ray and Leo were sprawled on chairs and

Dad was pacing about dragging his fingers through his hair. There was no rehearsing taking place, but there was plenty of frowning.

It didn't take long to work out the cause – one of the Dugongs was missing.

"Where *is* he?" Dad asked the ceiling. "He should be here by now. Ray, try him again, for god's sake. It'd be nice if we could have a drummer for our first gig in twenty years."

Uncle Ray pulled out his mobile, but just as he did, it sprang to life in his hand and played the first few bars of 'Collision Course'.

"Yeah, Ray here. Jen? I was just about to call – what's keeping Mick?" A pause, then, "Car accident?" The silence in the room set like ice. Uncle Ray sat down on a chair and leant forward with the phone pressed to his ear. "Don't cry, Jen. What happened?" Everyone's eyes were glued on Uncle Ray. At one point he rubbed his forehead and squeezed the bridge of his nose. Finally he said, "Look, there's nothing any of us can do now. Don't blame yourself. I'll let the others know and get back to you. Take care, Jen." Uncle Ray clicked off his mobile.

Dad was first to speak. "Ray, what is it?"

"He's in hospital – badly bruised hand and three broken fingers. He's buggered – he can't even pick up a drumstick, let alone use one."

"But what happened?"

"Apparently just as they were about to set off, Jen accidentally slammed the car door on his hand."

"She *what*? How'd she manage that?"

"Not sure. Something about loading up the car and them being in a rush and it being dark… She's pretty upset about the whole thing."

"*She's* upset?" Dad said, looking around in amazement. "*She's* upset? What about us? What are we going to do now? We're on in 90 minutes and we haven't got a drummer."

"Ron, can't you get someone to fill in… just for tonight?"

Dad turned on Mum as if she'd suggested he fly around the room. "Fill in? Fill in? It's our first gig for twenty years. We've been rehearsing together for two solid months to get it right and now you're asking me if we can get someone to fill in – just like that? It's impossible. Tell her."

Mum looked at Uncle Ray and then at Leo.

They both glanced up for a moment and then went back to staring at their hands.

Dad saw the look of disappointment on Mum's face and spoke more softly. "It's impossible, love. No one can fill in at the last moment. It can't be done."

"So what are you going to do, then?"

"Well, I don't think we have much of a choice. We've got no drummer. I'm afraid we'll just have to… cancel. I mean, what else can we do?"

Everybody in the room felt the finality of Dad's words pressing down on them. Well, almost everybody.

"I'll do it."

Six sets of eyes converged on Razza. Six sets of ears thought they must have been hearing things.

Razza looked around at all of us. "I'll do it. I'll fill in," he said, smiling and bobbing his head to some inner beatbox.

He was my friend. He'd obviously lost his mind. It was up to me to speak to him. "Razz… Can you even *play* the drums?"

Razza scratched his chin with his index finger. "Play the drums? Would that be *important*?" Then he looked at me as if I had a brain the size of a microbe's backside.

"Of *course* I can play the drums. I've been playing since I was three. My old man was a drummer – his one talent. He left me his drum kit, remember?"

"Look… Orazio," Dad said with a grimacing sort of smile, "don't get me wrong – I appreciate the offer, I really do, but it's… ridiculous. No matter how long you've been playing, you don't know the songs or the arrangements – even a top pro drummer would struggle."

"But I *do* know the songs."

Dad looked as if he'd been cracked over the head with a baseball bat. "What? How?"

"I borrowed your cassette off Ishmael ages ago. I've been playing along with it at home. That's how I practise – I get new songs and work out the drum bit until I can play it just the same. I know all the songs on the album and I've sat in on a few rehearsals, so I pretty much know what you're doing with them."

Uncle Ray placed his big hand on Razza's shoulder. "Son, playing along with a record in your bedroom to your pet goldfish is a bit different from playing on stage in front of hundreds of people."

"Yeah, I know. I played in front of a few hundred

people last weekend. When was the last time *you* did that?"

Uncle Ray's eyes narrowed. I was worried his big hand might slip to Razza's throat.

"Look, I play drums in my Uncle Aldo's band every fortnight down at the Italian Club. We get pretty big crowds down there. And when other singers and stuff come in we're the backing band as well, so we have to play everything from Dean Martin and Frank Sinatra through to the 1960s and 1970s and all the modern stuff. Sometimes there's hardly any time for rehearsal at all – you gotta just pick things up quick. I'm used to it."

Uncle Ray studied Razza closely then stepped back and made a sweeping gesture with his hand towards the drum kit. "All right, Keith Moon – show us your stuff."

Razza bounced across the room and adjusted the seat with a spin. Then he pulled some of the smaller drums and cymbals closer and picked up the sticks and twirled them through his fingers the way I had seen him do with his pens a thousand times in class. Three heavy booms came from the bass drum then he clattered the sticks across the smaller ones, ending with a cymbal clash.

"Cool, not a bad set. What would you like to hear?"

"Well, let's start off easy. Give us 'All the Time'," Uncle Ray said.

Razza started on the cymbals then moved into a slow steady beat. "That's pretty much it all the way through, except for this bit," he said, changing the rhythm slightly.

Leo was next. "Okay, what about 'Bad Day for Angels'?"

This time Razza began quietly then built steadily into a trickier rhythm. He stopped when Dad held up a hand.

"Do 'Collision Course', then."

"Cool!" Razza said, clubbing the drums with four thunderous beats before pausing and pointing a drumstick at Dad – "That's when you scream, Mr Leseur" – and then plunging into a hard driving beat that invaded your body and took over your muscles so that you couldn't help but move to its commands.

It was back to Uncle Ray. "All right, superstar, give us 'Dead Toad Society Blues'."

Immediately Razz launched into a throbbing tidal wave of rhythm. If that wasn't impressive enough, he stopped after a while and said, 'That's the way it is on the album, anyway, but I reckon it's a bit slow. It should be more like...' and then he played it again like a runaway bullet train with his hands blurring and the heavy bass drum thudding so loud you could feel your internal organs bouncing to the beat. It all ended with a roaring drum roll, after which Razza twirled a stick in his right hand and flung it into the air. I'm sure he would have caught it as well – if it hadn't embedded itself deep in a styrofoam panel in the ceiling.

Uncle Ray was still watching the drumstick dangling above Razza's head when he said, "We might stay with the original tempo, Sunshine... if you don't mind."

"Sure," Razza said, "I'm cool with that. I guess you older dudes might have trouble keeping up, hey?"

As someone with quite a lot of experience in these situations, I was fairly confident that, judging by the expression on Uncle Ray's face, he was imagining himself force-feeding a certain person an entire drum kit a piece at a time – and not all of it via the mouth.

Mum broke the silence. "Well? What do you say, Ron? I'm no expert, but that sounded *pretty* good to me. Orazio could do it, couldn't he – just for tonight?"

My father's face was clouded with doubt and fear.

"Look, he's good enough – very good – but there's more to it than that. We haven't practised together. There's the chemistry, the vibe of the band. And we're doing some covers as well – what about those? There's too much at stake. It's our first performance in twenty years. I just think it would be… safer… if we cancelled tonight. Maybe we could try again another time. People would understand… They'd have to. That's what I think, anyway." There was a long pause, then Dad added, "But The Dugongs have always done things as a team… So if you guys want to go ahead… then that's what we'll do."

Everyone looked at Leo. "I'm not waiting another twenty years."

We took that as a 'yes'.

Mum's face brightened a little. "Ray? What about you?"

Uncle Ray slumped back on his chair. "So it all comes down to me, does it? The future of The Dugongs is in my hands. Do we pack our bags and go home or do we pin our hopes on Superboy here? Big call. Well… for what it's worth… I agree with Ronnie."

Heads fell around the room – even Dad's –

and everyone just seemed to get smaller. Mum couldn't hide her disappointment. "Ray... are you sure?"

"About agreeing with Ronnie? Absolutely. I really think it would be *far* safer if we cancelled." Uncle Ray slowly looked around at everyone in the room. "... And *that's* why I say we should go with the kid."

Dad's head jerked up. "What? But you just said..."

"That it would be safer if we cancelled? That's right. But Ronnie, tell me, when have The Dugongs ever been about feeling safe? Geez, you'll be telling me that I should be relaxed and comfortable next."

Mum closed her eyes and put her fingers to her lips and Uncle Ray continued. "Remember when we first started playing? Don't know about you, but I felt about as safe as Keanu Reeves in that *Speed* movie, just flying along by the seat of my brown boxers. Ronnie, I've felt safe for the past twenty years. And you know what? I'm tired of safe. Sick of it. Now I'm ready for something else – I'm ready to feel alive even if it means being scared shitless. Hey, isn't that what playing with the 'Gongs is all about in the first place? Feeling alive. And look at it this way, Ronnie. Even if it all ends in some gigantic bus wreck, at least we'll have had one helluva wild ride, won't we? And I'll guarantee you, whatever happens, it'll sure beat the crap out of selling insurance."

Then Uncle Ray turned his craggy face to Razza. "Just one condition, though. If motormouth here stuffs up, just *once*, I get to be first in line to boot him up the arse, all right?"

"I'm second," Leo said.

We all waited for Dad.

"Well… I guess I'll just have to settle for third," he said.

"Hallelujah!" Mum cried, throwing back her head.

Razza celebrated with a machine gun burst on the drums. "What d'ya know?" he said, beaming his smile around the room like a lighthouse. "I'm a Dugong!"

Prue rolled her eyes and grinned wryly. "Was there ever any doubt?" she said.

43.
Sliced Open and
Pinned to a Board

Mum, Prue and I left the band to their fast and furious rehearsal and returned to the gym to pass on the news about the line-up change. First we told Mrs Zorzotto, who assured us that, "My Orazio won't let anyone down," and then we told Mr Barker, who stared back at us as if we'd informed him that Ronald McDonald had just been elected prime minister.

When the first of the school bands started up, Mum, Mrs Zorzotto and Mr Barker moved outside so, as they put it, they could hear themselves think. Prue and I hung around at the back of the gym, but we weren't by ourselves for long.

"There you are – look who I've found." It was Sally, and standing stiffly beside her like a little soldier was James Scobie. "Hi," she said, noticing Prue. "I'm Sally." Prue introduced herself and then Sally looked around. "Where's Razz?"

At first Sally seemed excited when I told her about Razza and the band, but then she had second thoughts. "Wait a minute. That means I've been stood up again. Who am I going to dance with now?" Then she pointed a finger at me. "This is all your fault, Ishmael. Your father's band has kidnapped my date. For your punishment, you'll have to dance with me instead."

As punishments go that was right up there with being force-fed chocolate. There was just one problem.

"I'd love to, Sal, I really would, but Razza asked me to get something for him at one of the stalls and bring it down to the rehearsal room. I've got to do that first."

Sally took a deep breath. "Scobie, what about you? You'll dance with me, won't you?"

Scobie's eyes flicked over to Prue and his mouth stretched in the opposite direction. "Well, certainly, I…"

But that was as far as he got before Prue reached over and grabbed him by the shirt front. "Sorry," she said with a sympathetic smile at Sally, "he's taken," and dragged him off towards the stage.

Sally looked daggers at me. "Well, I'm waiting."

I searched the crowd for a familiar face. I was about to give up when I spotted one lurking in the shadows by the back door. I ran over and grabbed him.

"Sally Nofke – this is Bill Kingsley from our debating team. Bill, this is Sally."

For a second Sally seemed a little overwhelmed by how much of Bill there actually was. Then she turned to me. "Not the famous Bill Kingsley? The one you told us about? The hero of last year's secret topic debate? The guru of sci-fi?"

"In the flesh," I said, then sort of wished I hadn't.

Sally smiled up at him. "Bill," she said, "I don't suppose you'd like to dance with me?"

It was a stupid question. Bill Kingsley was gazing back at her as if all his *Star Wars* had come at once. I left them together and headed off. By the time I returned from the rehearsal room, the second of the school bands was already playing. From the side door I surveyed the sea of bobbing heads, looking for Bill and Sally. Eventually I found them. They were dancing in a group with Prue and Scobie… and Kelly and Brad.

I watched them all for a moment, but every time Brad and Kelly laughed or smiled at each other or touched, something tore inside me like I was being stretched out another notch on a rack. In the end I decided there was no point in torturing myself, so I left to find a quiet place outside to wait until it was time for The Dugongs.

I ended up behind the gym on a low retaining wall around a garden bed and settled in to listen to the music. I was still there when the second of the school bands finished up and a short break was announced before the final support act would take the stage. A handful of people drifted out my way, but most hung around inside or headed for the playground and the food and drink stalls. I was thinking about going there myself when a shadow fell at my feet.

"So this is where you've been hiding. You're in big trouble, you know." Kelly Faulkner was framed by the glow of the gym lights behind her. It shone through the tips of her hair and outlined her body. She looked like some kind of angel – but what else was new?

"Trouble? Why?"

"Sally says you've been hiding just to get out of

dancing with her." She smiled half-heartedly and looked down at a beaded bag she was carrying. "I haven't thanked you for sending the tickets. That was nice... thanks."

"That's okay. I'm... glad you came. I wasn't sure if you would... you know, after..."

She looked at me and just nodded to show she understood what I was talking about. I knew it wouldn't do any good, but I couldn't stop the words from leaving my mouth.

"Kelly... I'm sorry, I really am. What I did... that was... stupid... Wrong."

Then she asked the question that I'd already asked myself a million times. "So... why did you do it?"

"I... I don't know."

But I did know and when I saw the hurt hiding in her eyes, I knew that whatever happened I needed to tell her the truth, no matter how much it scared me. I was just like Uncle Ray. I was tired of safe. Sick of it. "I just... I just wanted to know... if you... liked me or not."

Kelly tilted her head slightly as if she hadn't understood.

"I wasn't reading it all... really... I just wanted to

know what you wrote about me... So I'd know if you liked me or not."

"If you wanted to know that... why couldn't you just ask me?"

There was no way I could explain to someone like Kelly Faulkner how impossible that was for someone like me, so I just shook my head.

There was a long silence and then I heard her step closer, followed by the sound of a zip and a shuffle of pages.

"Here."

When I looked up she was holding her diary out to me. It was open.

"No... I don't want..."

"Go on. You said you wanted to know what I wrote about you. Well here it is. It's all right – I want you to read it."

I took the diary from her. It was open at the same page I had started to read that day at her house.

ISHMAEL

I always thought Ishmael was a nice guy especially after what he did for Marty – though I must admit, some pretty weird things seem to happen to him – eg Sally's pool! But now that I've got to know him a bit better, I think that he's…

I glanced up as Kelly then turned the page.

… really nice and funny and the kind of boy you can trust.

All of a sudden I felt like one of those dissected toads in the science lab – sliced open and pinned to a board. If Mr Guthrie was right and one day the words would find me, I was praying it would be now. But my words must have lost their compass and marched off a cliff somewhere.

It was Kelly who spoke first. "And I found… this… in the diary."

She handed a small slip of paper to me.

The words 'Hot or what!' screamed up at me. I couldn't believe it. It was back! It should have been dead and buried long ago, but every time I thought I'd pounded down the last spadeful of soil on its grave, it shoved its hands up through the dirt and came for me again. It was possessed! It was unstoppable! Maybe Mr Guthrie was right all along. Maybe Razza's poem really was "rigid with rigor mortis" and that's why you could never kill it – because it was already dead! Yes, that was it. The horrible truth hit me as I stared at the paper in my hands and the words seemed to crawl off the page like a swarm of shiny black beetles. It was poetry's answer to *The Mummy* – and now it was after Kelly!

Luckily a soft voice eventually hooked me back to something approaching reality. "Is it… Did *you*… write it?"

It was like being accused of emptying my bladder in the pool all over again.

"No… No way… You don't think… No, it's not mine… That's all Razza's work… He gave it to me… He was just trying to help… I… I had it in my hand when… It must've got caught inside by mistake… but I didn't write it… Really… I would never write something like that about you… I wouldn't… No way… I just wouldn't."

Kelly held up a hand like she was stopping traffic and gave a little grimace. "It's all right. I believe you. I believe you."

"I would never write something like that about you – not ever," I said again, just to make certain.

Kelly nodded thoughtfully and I was pretty sure I'd convinced her that Razza's poem had nothing to do with me, but then a doubt flickered across her face. The movement of her head slowly ground to a halt. She frowned and squinted at me through one eye. "You'd never write something like that about me? So... what are you saying? That you... *don't* think I'm hot?"

Wild thoughts erupted in my head like a flock of startled birds. I frantically tried to catch some of them. "Well, yes... but... no... Well, not *no*... I mean, of course you're... You know... but not like *that*... Well you *are*... but it's just... you're... You're..."

I looked up quickly. I thought I saw a smile hiding on Kelly's face, but I must have been mistaken. I tried one last time to say something that didn't sound like I was a baboon with an anvil for a tongue stud.

"You're... You're everything that poem says... More... You really are, I mean it... A lot more... It's just... I don't know... I just think... that that's the *least* of what you are."

What? Did that come out right? Did it even make sense? Had I just insulted Kelly Faulkner? I forced myself to look up. She was gazing at me as if she couldn't believe what she had just heard. This was bad. I wondered if Kelly had a right hook like Barry Bagsley's. It didn't look like I would have to wait long to find out.

She took another step closer. I braced myself. Then she spoke in a whisper. "That's probably…"

Oh no – here it comes.

Circle the most appropriate response:

"That's probably…

    (a)   the most offensive

    (b)   the most childish

    (c)   the stupidest

    (d)   the creepiest

… thing anyone has ever said to me."

Kelly paused as if she was making her choice. Then she continued. "… The most…"

Somebody save me! Where's the cavalry when you need them? Where's the Man of Steel? Hey, now would be a great time for an earthquake to hit or that volcano to blow. Anyone for an alien invasion? If someone's out there – come on down! Please, give me something – anything! I want my knight in shining armour!

"Hey, Kel. Whatcha doing? I got the drinks."

Over by the doorway Brad was holding up two plastic cups. Thank you, Captain America! You just saved my life!

"Ishmael – didn't see you there. How're you going? Thanks for the tickets. Can't wait to hear your dad's band. Hey, you coming in, Kel? They're about to start up again."

For some reason Kelly seemed a little confused. "Oh… right… Sorry. Just give us a second, okay? Won't be long."

Brad shrugged and wandered back inside.

Kelly waited till he was gone then turned back to me. "Well… I um… I have to go… You know…"

I did know. Brad was waiting.

"Are you coming in?"

"No… I think I'll just hang around here till Dad's on."

"Okay, but don't forget you still owe Sally a dance sometime."

Kelly turned and drifted towards the gym as if she didn't really want to get there. She was almost at the entrance before I became aware of the velvety feel of the book in my hands.

"Kelly," I called, holding up the diary, "you forgot this."

I took it over to her and she looked at it for a few seconds before she spoke. "Could you do me a favour?" she said. "This… can be a bit of a pain… You know, carrying it around and trying to dance and everything. So… if you're staying out here anyway… maybe you could… mind it for me? Just for a little while – just until you come in?"

Kelly Faulkner held me captive in her crystal eyes.

"Yeah… Yeah, of course… But… are you *sure*?"

"I'm sure," she said.

I took the diary back and grasped it tightly with both hands.

"I'll take good care of it… I promise."

Kelly nodded. "I know you will," was all she said.

44.
Twenty Years in the Making

When Kelly left, I sat back down and looked at the diary in my hands. It contained all of her secret thoughts and her most private moments, and I knew that if I sat there for the rest of my life I would never look inside.

I turned over to the back cover and, with my finger, wrote my initials above Kelly's in the soft red suede and traced the outline of a heart around them both. Then I moved my hand slowly across the surface and swept it all away.

I was still sitting there listening to the music and thinking about Kelly Faulkner when a flash of light beyond the roof of the gym caught my eye. A few seconds later a murmur of thunder crept in from the distance. It sounded like we might be in for a storm. I hoped not. It would spoil the night a bit.

Of course I could always blame Kelly, I thought – her father *was* the weatherman after all. Poor Kelly. I wondered if anyone ever thanked her when the weather was good. Probably not. It was a tough gig being the daughter of a weatherman.

And that's what I was thinking about when some words found me at last. They may not have been Shakespeare or even Zorzotto, but they were me… and they were true. So I used the little thin pen from the spine of Kelly's diary and the space on the back of Razza's poem, and I wrote them down.

I'd only just finished when a howl of whistles and cheers spilled from the gym as the lights dimmed. Quickly sliding the sheet back into Kelly's diary I moved inside where a mass of people were surging towards the stage. Then a voice blared over the PA and everyone from St Daniel's instinctively froze in fear.

It was Mr Barker, but this time we had nothing to worry about. "Ladies and Gentlemen, it's been twenty years too long, but tonight, live on stage, St Daniel's

College, in association with 8 Triple N, is proud to present… the triumphant return of The Dugongs!"

Then the lights blazed on and the crowd erupted as Dad, Uncle Ray and Leo stood arm-in-arm on stage while a huge banner by Ms Lagilla's art class of a guitar-playing dugong was unfurled behind them.

After that Dad introduced each of the band members. When it was Razza's turn he said, "And making a surprise special guest appearance for one night only, on drums, Orazio 'The Razzman' Zorzotto!" The crowd whooped and clapped as Razza climbed up on to his stool and raised his arms in the air like Rocky Balboa – except I don't remember Rocky ever wearing a Pi-Man T-shirt with the sleeves cut out.

Then Dad's voice boomed around the hall. "This concert is for Billy."

Razza nodded to the rest of the band and pounded out four thudding beats to signal the start of 'Collision Course'. In front of him Leo and Uncle Ray kicked in with a wail of guitars and Dad grabbed the mike in both hands and let out a scream that sounded like it had been twenty years in the making.

All around me the crowd bounced and throbbed to

Razza's thumping beat, and even though I knew that somewhere among all those gyrating bodies Kelly Faulkner was with someone else, just at that moment it didn't seem important. All that mattered was that Razza was attacking the drums as if he was Bruce Lee, Uncle Ray and Leo were prowling around the stage with smiles as wide as their guitars and Dad was singing his lungs out and leaping about like some crazy kid. It was enough to make you feel like laughing and cheering and pumping your fists into the air all at the same time. And that's exactly what I did.

In the words of the Razzman, it was time to "par-taaaay". And why not? The Dugongs had finally returned, and they'd brought my father with them.

45.
The Top Ten

The Top Ten things I'll always remember about The Dugongs' Twenty Year Reunion Concert:

1. *Dancing with Sally Nofke* after she dragged me up to join the others and told me that I had to take my punishment with a smile... which I did.
2. *Hearing The Dugongs play their first song in front of a live audience for twenty years* and being deafened by the roar that followed.
3. *Every song after that.*
4. *Salty dancing with Bill* and thinking it was like watching a beautiful dark moon orbiting an enormous smile.

5. *Prue laughing hysterically* as Scobie performed his own unique style of dancing, which consisted of absolutely no movement at all except for some random shoulder hunching and an occasional wiggle of the hips.

6. *My mum crying* and pressing her fingers against her lips like she was praying when Dad sat alone on stage with an acoustic guitar and sang a new song dedicated to Billy Mangan called 'Memory sea' and me knowing who I would go to if I ever needed help with a poem.

7. *Razza looking horrified when he spotted his mother and Mr Barker dancing together* and how quickly he changed when he saw how happy she looked.

8. *The ten-minute encore performance of 'Dead Toad Society Blues'* that Razza had cranked up to warp speed until Uncle Ray and Leo exchanged a wink and boosted it up even further and continued to power it along while Dad ran into the crowd and pulled Mum and Mr Barker and Mrs Zorzotto up on stage as backing singers to blast out the chorus, which had the entire audience dancing and bouncing around like a giant beast until it all came to a dramatic end when Razza

thrashed out an insane, head-banging drum solo, then made a final desperate lunge at a cymbal that shattered his drumstick and sent him tumbling from his stool and crashing to the stage.

9. *The band taking their final bows* with everyone throwing streamers and waving glow sticks and going crazy and Uncle Ray calling Razza over and yanking his arm into the air like he was world champion while behind them Mrs Zorzotto whooped and cheered and bounced up and down, jabbing Mr Barker in the ribs with her elbow until he grimaced as if he couldn't believe what he was about to do, then raised his hands above his head, clapped them together and gave Razza the thumbs up.

10. *Dad standing up on stage* waving to everyone and laughing and joking with the band and hugging Mum and spinning her round so that her feet twirled above the floor.

Yes, they were definitely my concert highlights all right. But the night wasn't over yet, and there were other highlights still to come.

One of them would be the highlight of my entire year.

Track 9:
The Very Best
of Everything

There were times when the walls came down
Times when the bells rang out
Times when the cavalry came through.
There were times when we read the signs
Times when we held the line
And the very best of everything was you.

From The Dugongs: *Returned & Remastered*
Music & lyrics: R. Leseur

46.
The Weatherman's Daughter

The Return of The Dugongs concert turned out to be one of the most successful events ever held at St Daniel's Boys College.

Apart from the healthy ticket sales, the Parents and Friends did a roaring trade on the food and drink stalls, the car park was all profit and the *Return of The Dugongs* commemorative T-shirts sold out, with orders for over a hundred more. I even passed a group of girls all wearing Pi-Men T-shirts and going on about the "hot drummer".

The Dugongs themselves couldn't have asked for a better response. Some club owners had come along to check them out, and after the concert there were offers for more gigs next year, and a man from a record company talked about a remastering of the original album. When Dad asked him if he would like to meet "our manager", Mr Barker did that smiling thing again. But he wasn't alone.

There were a lot of smiles being shared around me that night – Prue and Scobie, Mum and Dad, Mr Barker and Mrs Zorzotto and, of course, Sally and Razza – that is, until I turned around and found that they had mysteriously disappeared. They weren't the only ones. Kelly and Brad also seemed to have vanished somewhere. I really didn't want to think about that. So with Dad and the band still surrounded by a crush of well-wishers and autograph hunters, I decided to escape to the playground.

Outside, there were still lots of people standing around talking excitedly, packing up gear or threading their way down to the car park. Over by one of the stalls I spotted Miss Tarango. She was wearing a *Return of The Dugongs* T-shirt tied in a knot at the side. She was with Mr Guthrie. They were struggling to carry a long rolled-up canvas tarpaulin, but every time they

tried to pick it up it sagged in the middle and then
Miss would laugh so much that she would lose all her
strength and drop it. Eventually, after a few attempts,
she seemed to go weak at the knees and just sat on the
tarp wiping tears from her eyes and holding her
stomach. Mr Guthrie just stared at her and shook his
head. I knew what he was thinking. That it just wasn't
possible to write a poem to match Miss Tarango.

I thought for a moment about giving them a hand
with the tarpaulin, but I guessed they didn't really need
me, so I made for my old spot by the retaining wall.
The only problem was, when I got there, I found
someone had beaten me to it.

A pair of eyes like soft, blue diamonds looked up
at me.

"Hey, Ishmael."

"Kelly…"

She smiled. "Sorry, I guess I stole your place, didn't I?"

"No problem. It's yours."

"Thanks."

Then there was one of those awkward silences that
seemed to stalk me wherever I go. Luckily a question
saved me. "How come…"

"I'm out here on my lonesome? Well, it seems it's my night for being abandoned," Kelly said with an exaggerated sigh. "First, my best friend runs off somewhere with this mad drummer and then my... then Brad... starts talking footy with his mates. What's a girl to do?"

We smiled at each other. I racked my brains to think of something else to say to keep the conversation going, but the 'awkward silence' stalker had cornered me again. Kelly looked at the bag that was on her lap and began picking at the beads.

"I *really* enjoyed the concert," she said. "Your dad is pretty cool."

"Yeah... I guess he gets it from me."

She giggled. I wished there was some way I could do that for a living – make Kelly Faulkner laugh.

"Yes... Well, you might be right there. After all, you've got that really cool nickname, haven't you... *Paddy*?"

"Ah... now *that* might have been a mistake."

"You *think*?" Kelly said in mock surprise.

This time the two of us laughed a little. Then the silence poured back in like sand into a hole and smothered us both.

Kelly looked down again at her bag and shook her head. "I still can't believe Razza, can you? Wasn't he... incredible? How could he do that – just come in at the last minute and everything?"

"Well, it's easy for him. He's a child of the universe, you know."

"Really?"

"Yep – he told me so himself."

Kelly grinned and nodded. "Now *that* I can believe." Then her eyes focused on something behind me. "Speak of the devil," she said.

I looked over my shoulder. At the far end of the playground Sally and Razza were standing together searching the crowd.

"I'd better get going. Sally's parents will be waiting for us at the car."

She stood up. We were facing each other.

"Well, thanks again for the tickets. I really had a fun night. And tell your dad I thought the band was great, okay?"

"Okay."

"So... I guess I'll see you around... with debating... or whatever..."

Kelly waited as if she expected me to say something. And I wanted to say something. I wanted to tell her not to go. I wanted to tell her that I didn't think I could survive till debating started next year before I saw her again. I wanted to tell her that there was no way I would ever talk football with my mates if I could talk to her instead. I wanted to tell her how great she was, how beautiful she looked. I wanted to tell her about her eyes and her smile and how I only felt alive when I was near her.

I opened my mouth to speak. "Okay," I said.

She gave a half-smile and moved past me. "Right... Well, I..." Then she stopped. "Oh... Wait... I almost forgot." She reached down into her bag, pulled out her diary and slid a small slip of paper from between its pages. "I thought maybe Razza might want his poem back – you know, that *maybe* now there's someone *special* he could give it to."

Kelly held out Razza's poem, but before I could take it, she frowned and slowly drew it back. Her head was bowed. She was staring at the four lines written in pencil on the other side. "What's this?" she said. I watched as Kelly's eyes traced the words on the page. When she'd finished she looked up at me for a moment then returned to the lines and read them aloud in her soft, creamy voice:

> *"The weatherman tells you if you ask him –*
> *Will it be rainy or will it be fine?*
> *The weatherman uses charts and tables,*
> *But the weatherman's daughter… makes the*
> *sun shine."*

I held my breath as she closed the diary gently around the poem and placed them both in her bag. Then she looked up and took a step forward. All I could see were her ice-blue eyes and all I could smell was her perfume. It crossed my mind that this would be a very bad time to pass out.

As I was trying not to think about that, Kelly placed her hands lightly on my shoulders, leaned forward and pressed her lips gently on mine. That's when the rest of the world disappeared and every cell in my body erupted in a massive Mexican wave. It was like suddenly discovering a hundred new levels to your favourite computer game, only better – *much* better.

It only lasted a second. Kelly stepped back, drew in a breath and exhaled slowly. I wanted to breathe too, but either I'd forgotten how or it just didn't seem necessary any more. She smiled and I felt like someone had speared a fence post through my heart.

"Now look what you made me do," she said.

She held up her palm and opened and shut her hand like a little Muppet. "'Bye Ishmael."

I tried to say goodbye back but apparently someone had removed my voice box and forgot to tell me.

Kelly was only a few paces away when she stopped, twirled around and held up her index finger. "By the power vested in me," she said in her best debating voice, "I hereby declare that tomorrow will be clear and sunny."

Then she gave a little bow and laughed.

It was the sound of the universe unfolding as it should.

47.
Just Crazy Enough
to be True

I sat down on the retaining wall in a daze as Kelly
headed across the playground towards Razza and
Sally. I watched as they chatted and laughed together
for a moment before Kelly pointed in my direction and
both the girls gave Razza a hug. Then Kelly grabbed
Sally's arm and they ran down the path that led to the
car park.

Seconds later Razza bounded in beside me.
"Maaaaaaate! What an awesome night, eh? Wicked!"
Even for Razza the smile on his face was enormous.
I thought for a moment about checking to see if it met
at the back of his head.

"Yeah, just a shame that Sally's not as smart as we thought she was."

"Hey? What d'ya mean?"

"Well, she's got the hots for you, hasn't she, so she can't be too bright, right?"

"Why you…" I found myself in a headlock while Razza pretended to throw wild punches at my skull. "Take that, you scumbag!" Suddenly he stopped. "Hey, I got something *huge* to tell you man, *huge*!"

"Yeah well, Razz, I've got something huge…"

But Razza's limited attention span had been deflected somewhere else.

"Prindabel! My mega main man!"

Ignatius was carrying a load of T-shirts across the playground. He flinched when he heard Razza's voice, then edged cautiously towards us as if he was approaching a dangerous beast.

When Razza leaped up Ignatius froze like a startled deer.

"That poem – I owe you big time, dude. Big time. You really came through, bro. Thanks loads, man," Razza said, spreading his arms wide.

Ignatius backed off in terror, holding his bundle

of shirts in front of him as if he was fending off an assault.

"Zorzotto, no! Back off! I did it for me – and everyone else – but mainly me. You're even more of a pain when you're depressed. You don't owe me anything – nothing at all."

Razza let his arms fall slowly to his side and nodded seriously at Ignatius. "Right... sure," he said. "No worries, man. I get it. You're just not into open displays of affection. I understand. I'm totally cool with that."

An uneasy feeling of déjà vu crept over me.

"Although..." Razz said, peeking up slyly, "could I *just* do this?"

And before Ignatius could react, Razza had grabbed his head, yanked it forward and planted a long juicy kiss on Prindabel's high, wide forehead complete with appropriate sound effects.

"Mmmmmmmmmmmmwwwwwwwwwwaaaaaaaa!"

When he was finally released, Ignatius reeled back as if he'd been shot, and a mulberry-coloured circle like a bullet hole began darkening in the middle of his brow.

"That poem, man... I take it all back, Prindabuddy.

You're not a nerd at all, dude – you're way cool. Man, you're so cool, I could fill you up with water and use you for an ice tray."

Ignatius had the same expression on his face that I'm sure a certain Doctor Frankenstein wore when he discovered that bringing something back to life is not without its risks. He turned to me. The plea of 'Do something!' was screaming in his eyes.

I shrugged my shoulders and smiled at him.

Razza rapped him on the chest. "You and me, Iggy. I'm telling you, dude, we're blood."

Ignatius gave a sickly grin then scuttled off as Razza shouted after him, "I love you man!"

Then he spun back around. "Now wait till you hear my awesome news – it's about Kelly."

"Well actually, I've got something…"

"Just wait up, dude," Razza said, thumping his hand on my shoulder. "Before you go crapping on about how you got no chance with Kelly and how nothing will ever happen with the two of you because she's perfect and you're a lump of wood, at least listen to what I've got to say, okay?"

"But that's…"

"Aaaaaaahhh!" Razza said, clamping his hand over my mouth. "Just *listen*, okay?"

I closed my eyes and nodded helplessly and he took his hand away.

"Dude, you are so going to love this. Sally says that Brad and Kelster are splitting up. That's right. It's history, man. She reckons they don't have much in common or something. Apparently they're still gonna be friends and everything, but tonight was sort of like the final fling. Anyway, I don't reckon old Brad will be too cut up, because Sal says Kelly's setting him up with Jess, who apparently is chomping at the bit. So mate, that's not just a window of opportunity – that's a Grand Canyon of opportunity! And you know what else?"

I rocked my head from side to side.

"Poetry, mate – it works!"

"Yeah, but wait until—"

I found myself slapped in another mouth clamp.

"For once in your life just listen to me, dude. I know what I'm talking about. I've got first-hand experience. Prindabel's poem, mate – it worked, it *really* worked. Miss Tarango was right. Chicks dig poetry. I'm telling you, man, if we can just come up with the right poem for Kelly, you'd be in mate, you'd be definitely in!"

A pair of high-beam eyes blazed at me. I peeled Razza's fingers off my mouth like they were octopus tentacles.

"So let me get this straight. What you're telling me is… that if I came up with the right poem… You think that I could actually win Kelly over?"

A head jiggled before me like a rabbit.

"You know what, Razz?" I said. "I reckon that's just crazy enough to be true."

He gawked at me in shock. "What… You mean… you actually *agree* with me… about Kelly… and poetry and everything?"

"Yep, I actually do… I guess you could say I'm totally cool with that."

For the first time in my life I'd taken the wind out of Razza's massive sail.

"Well… let's not get too carried away here. This poetry writing… it's tricky stuff, you know."

"Are you kidding me? Aren't you the Razzman, famous author of 'Hot or what!'?

"Well, yeah…"

"And am I or am I not Ishmael Leseur, the first-born

son of Ronnie 'The Red' Leseur, the Towering Inferno – lead singer and chief songwriter of The Dugongs?"

"You are…"

"Then who knows what we can do when we combine our super powers?"

Razza's eyes grew into plates. "Hey, that's right! That's absolutely right. You and me, man – the dynamic duo! Come on," he said, dragging me up. "We gotta get out of here. I just remembered, your folks have got the search party out for you. I told them you were probably making out in the dark with some hot chick."

I rolled my eyes and laughed. "Ha! That'll be the day."

"Soon, dude, soon," Razza said, pushing me ahead of him into the playground. "Just you wait. All we need is a wicked poem, and I've got some awesome ideas already. Like how's this for a killer rhyming omelette?"

Then he clasped both hands high on his chest and bellowed out into the night:

> *"I've got the hots for a chick called Kelly*
> *She's better to look at than the telly!"*

There was only one thing I could say to that as the

Razzman and I charged like lunatics towards the glowing lights of the gym.

"Rigid, dude! Totally rigid!"

48.
PS

PS Just in case you were wondering, Kelly Faulkner was wrong about the weather. When I woke up the next morning it was raining and it rained non-stop all day.

But not on me.

ACKNOWLEDGEMENTS

My heartfelt thanks go to all my family and friends but especially to my 'fabulous' wife Adriana and to Meg and Joe. Even if it was possible to do it without you guys, what would be the point?

I am forever in debt to the good folk at Scholastic Australia and the wonderful women at Omnibus Books for everything they have done and continue to do on my behalf. In particular, a super-sized thanks to my supportive and confidence-boosting publisher Dyan Blacklock and my hard-working and wise editor Celia Jellett.

Finally I'd like to give special and long overdue thanks to all my guitar buddies through the years – Rob, Steve, Greg, Bernie and Joe – who have helped make music such an important and joyous part of my life. Hey, maybe it's time for a reunion concert...

THE AUTHOR

When quizzed about his own memories of school, author Michael Gerard Bauer recollects three things clearly:

1. His ambition was to become a Samurai warrior.
2. Standing in front of his fellow students was as daunting a prospect for him as it is for Ishmael.
3. He never thought about writing.

Fortunately for his readers, soon after graduating from the University of Queensland, Michael quickly traded in his dreams of martial arts expertise, became a teacher and began to write.

Michael has since discovered that he is, after all, rather good at writing and has received a raft of awards for his *Ishmael* series, including the 2008 South Australian Festival Award for Literature and the 2007 Children's Peace Prize. In 2007 he was also shortlisted for the CBCA Award for Older Readers and the White Ravens festival at the Bologna Book Fair.

Michael now lives in the beautiful Brisbane suburb of Ashgrove with his family.

Don't miss the first hilarious *Ishmael* book:

Don't Call Me Ishmael

Michael Gerard Bauer

ISBN 978-1-84877-683-8
Also available as an ebook
ISBN 978-1-84877-685-2 (mobi)
ISBN 978-1-84877-686-9 (epub)

There's no easy way to put this, so I'll say it straight out. It's time I faced up to the truth. I'm fourteen years old and I have Ishmael Leseur's Syndrome. There is no cure.

'Comic genius and a great read.'
The Bookseller

'Sharp and witty... utterly engaging.'
Marilyn Brocklehurst, Norfolk Children's Book Centre

'An extremely funny book that doesn't shy away from the inevitable growing pains of adolescence.'
Staff Picks, Foyles